The Labcoat

For Michelle Schwartz —
Thanks for your help
with this.

Larry Soderquist

The Labcoat

An Eric Berg Mystery

HILLSBORO PRESS
Franklin, Tennessee

Printed in the United States of America

02 01 00 99 98 1 2 3 4 5

Library of Congress Catalog Card Number: 98–65597

ISBN: 1-57736-088-5

Dust jacket design by Gary Bozeman
Dust jacket photographs © 1998 by Hans H. Soderquist

Grateful acknowledgment is made to George J. Fruhman, of the Albert Einstein School of Medicine, for permission to reprint a portion of his poem, "The Anatomy Lesson," copyright © 1978 by the author. All rights reserved.

Published by
HILLSBORO PRESS
an imprint of
PROVIDENCE HOUSE PUBLISHERS
238 Seaboard Lane • Franklin, Tennessee 37067
800-321-5692

To my colleagues,
both faculty and administration,
who try with me to understand the interrelationships
among law, morality, and justice and
who struggle along with me over issues confronting
the modern research university.

Prologue

FRANK WILLARD BEGAN TRUDGING UP THE BACK STAIRS. SINCE HE CARRIED 200 pounds on a 160-pound frame, and had walked down a long hallway with an armload of books, he already felt strain. When he reached the landing between floors, the door above him opened, and someone with a newspaper started down. At first Willard didn't notice who it was, but then he did, and he smiled thinly and mumbled hello.

As they came nearer, Willard wondered why the person was crowding him, almost shoving the newspaper in his face. Then the newspaper exploded, startling Willard and making him suck in his breath. His head began to spin, and as the person who had crowded him hurried past with the newspaper still in hand, Willard was surprised to see that the newspaper was all in one piece.

Cocking his head in confused curiosity, Willard wondered about the newspaper and at the same time wondered why he couldn't breathe. Or rather, though he could breathe, why it didn't do him any good. As he fell, what seemed important to Willard was keeping his hold on the books, because his last image was of his second grade teacher telling him that books should not be hurt.

Chapter One

Eric Berg leaned back in his black, high-backed chair, his feet propped on the corner of the big walnut desk that dominated his office. An autumn storm had just passed, and he studied the columns of sunlight that streaked through breaks in the dark, rolling clouds.

As he gazed out the window, his telephone rang. "We've got a problem at the chemistry building," the university patrolman began. "One of the professors collapsed on the stairs, and I can't get him moved."

"Why not?" Berg asked, as he plopped his feet back on the floor.

The patrolman let out what to Berg seemed a frustrated sigh. "The ambulance people say they can't take him to the emergency room on their own say-so, because he was dead when they got here."

"Have you called the city police?"

"Yessir. The detective sergeant told me his people are tied up."

"A typical Friday afternoon," Berg said with a hint of resignation.

"Yeah, payday. Anyway, the sergeant wants us to do a quick look around and get some pictures, then they'll pick things up after the body is at the medical examiner's."

"I'll come over."

"Good," the patrolman said, sounding relieved that his problem had been solved. "Stairs between the fifth and sixth floors."

"I'm on my way." Berg started to put the phone down, then had another thought. "Who found the body?"

"One of the secretaries."

"Don't let her get away. I'll want to talk to her. Also, ask any bystanders if they saw anything."

"Already did. Nothing."

After college, Berg had been a military police officer in Vietnam. In the years since, he'd gone through Princeton Seminary and done a Ph.D. at Yale before serving for a couple of years as the pastor of a fashionable church in New Haven. Then, when he thought the time was right, he'd joined the Divinity School faculty at Mellon University, where the sign on his door now read "Professor of Theology." Even though he was only in his forties, Berg was one of the handful of first-rate systematic theologians in the country, and Mellon was a top twenty research university—its main rival being Duke, which was a hundred miles away. The shelves nearest Berg's desk sagged from the books and articles he had written. Most of his work was highly praised, and what wasn't should have been.

A couple of years ago, though, Berg began to miss his duty as a young lieutenant in Saigon, and that, along with the boredom of middle age, had led him to become the university police chaplain. One day he defused a standoff between the police and a drugged-up graduate student who was holed up in an apartment with a shotgun. Berg did this by foolishly—as he thought about it later—standing in front of the police and saying through a bullhorn, "I'll pray with you, I'll pray for you, or I'll pray over you, but let's not take all day to decide. Do I tell these people to start shooting, or what?"

After that, the chief of police began asking Berg to do more and more for the department, and a year ago the department had made him an assistant chief—big title, no salary. He helped out as they needed and as he had time, which suited everybody.

BEFORE LEAVING HIS OFFICE ON HIS WAY TO THE CHEMISTRY building, Berg lifted the top of his battered attaché case and slipped out his revolver—a Smith & Wesson Chief's Special, .38 caliber, five shots and a two-inch barrel. He rarely wore the gun around school, but he always put it on before he walked out of the building. The university wasn't in the safest of neighborhoods, and it was dangerous to carry a badge and not a gun, because the badge brought responsibilities that couldn't be backed away from.

Berg had to contort himself to slide his six-foot-two-inch body into the old Corvette he enjoyed owning, but did not much enjoy driving. As he was reminded daily, including on the short drive to the chemistry building, it was not the most practical car. He flicked the car's leather-covered steering wheel left and then sharply right, missing potholes that would have pounded his back, as he pulled into the parking lot outside the building. Unlike most of the campus, the chemistry building wasn't ivy-covered, old red brick. It was utilitarian sixties modern, tan brick and glass, six stories high.

Berg rode the elevator up five floors and walked to the other end of the building, wondering what he would find beyond what the patrolman had told him. It was easy to spot the stairwell because of the crowd that had gathered. He pulled out his credentials case and stuck it in the outside breast pocket of his blazer, letting the side with the badge hang out. He shouldered his way through the crowd and entered the stairwell.

"Thanks for coming, Chief," the patrolman said.

"No problem. Let's see what we've got. Anything been moved?"

"No, sir. This is the way I found things. The medics didn't have to move anything to see what they needed to."

"Who is he?"

"Frank Willard. One of the chemistry professors. Had an office and lab on the sixth floor. Looks like that's where he was headed."

Berg found the scene in the stairwell strangely discordant. He had never seen a person, or much of anything else, lying on a stairway. And as he could see, lying on a stairway didn't work too well. Willard was on his stomach, but turned slightly so that Berg, standing on the left side of the stairs going up, could see some of Willard's upper left chest and the left side of his face. The professor had obviously slid down about two steps from where he fell, because the books he seemed to have been carrying, all chemistry textbooks of some sort, were now slightly above his head, still pretty much neatly together, with Willard's arms stretched out toward them.

Willard had been in his mid-to-late fifties and Caucasian. Hair, brown with gray streaks. Overweight. The dead man had on a blue oxford cloth shirt with a white labcoat on top, dark blue washpants, and rubbersoled Rockport shoes. All neat and clean.

Berg carefully set down his worn gray camera bag and knelt by Willard's body, so he could get a better look. As he did he momentarily slipped back into his old role as pastor and silently said a prayer for the dead professor.

"Looks like a heart attack," Berg said to the university patrolman, "judging by the bluish red tint of his skin."

Berg knew he was showing off, but he couldn't resist playing the expert in front of a university patrolman who usually dealt only with live bodies who merely snuck beer on campus and parked their cars in faculty lots. In fact, Berg's knowledge of how a heart attack victim looks was limited to one incident, the collapse of an embassy press secretary in Saigon a long time before.

"Still," Berg went on, "I guess we better do something."

He checked the body the best he could without moving it, looking for anything out of the ordinary, but found nothing. The professor's eyes were just barely open, as if he were sneaking a peek out of them.

Berg pulled the wallet from Willard's left rear pants pocket, counted fifty-four dollars in bills, and put the wallet back where he found it.

Berg gazed around the stairwell, searching for anything out of place. Nothing. Just an institutional-green stairwell with concrete block walls, steel-capped concrete steps, and two black handrails. As he looked at the landings at each end and midway between the floors, he noticed a slight smell of something he wasn't used to. But since this was the chemistry building, Berg expected unusual smells.

"Okay," he said. "Let me get some pictures, and then we'll turn him over."

For the next five minutes Berg shot photos with the old Nikon F he'd first learned to use in his off-duty hours in Saigon. He worked systematically, as he did everything, starting with a shot up the stairwell through the open fifth floor door, then from various spots going up the stairs, and then through the open sixth floor door and at points coming down. He finished with a series of close-ups of Willard's body, taken from different angles.

Three of Berg's shots were for no other reason than to include in a picture the patrolman, Tommy Allbright, and the two ambulance medics who waited at the bottom of the steps. The film he used came only in thirty-six exposure rolls, and though he didn't need a whole roll to record the scene in the stairwell, he was going to have the roll developed that afternoon anyway. Police and medics liked to have pictures of themselves on the job, and it didn't cost anything to accommodate them.

"Okay, that's enough for me," Berg said. "Let's turn him over."

Berg and Allbright, along with the two medics, pulled Willard's body to the middle of the stairway as they turned it on its back. Then Berg looked again and found nothing. He took his last three pictures, getting close-ups of this side of the body, and began to put his camera away, motioning to the medics with a wave of his hand that they could load Willard's body on their cart.

"You're taking him to University Hospital?" Berg asked.

"Yessir."

"Who's handling the emergency room end of things?"

"The detective sergeant downtown has that covered," Allbright answered. "He's calling to tell the emergency room to send the body to the medical examiner's once they log it in DOA."

"That's good. It's city's case now. But I still need to talk to the secretary who found the body."

"I'll go get her."

A minute later Berg saw the patrolman walking toward him with a short, thin woman of about twenty-three, who looked nervous, or more likely excited, Berg thought. Since Vietnam, he hadn't often seen that reaction, and it carried his mind back.

"Chief, this is Marilyn Harris," Allbright said, interrupting Berg's thoughts. "She found the body."

In a couple of minutes Berg had her story. She had walked through the sixth floor door and found Willard and his books, just as they were, she said, when Allbright arrived a few minutes later. "How close did you get to Willard?" Berg asked, and she said, "Just close enough to see that he wasn't breathing, and that his face was a funny blue color." Berg knew the rest.

"What can we do with the books?" Berg asked.

"I'll get some help, and we'll put them in his office," Marilyn Harris volunteered.

"Tommy, lend a hand, will you, and then get Ms. Harris to put what she told us in a statement."

"You've got it."

The Labcoat

On his way home, Berg stopped at a one-hour photo shop and ordered prints from his roll of film, saying he'd pick them up Monday morning. Nothing to do until then.

As he steered his car through the Friday rush-hour traffic, Berg felt an exhilaration he hadn't experienced since his days as a young army lieutenant. Now that he was in his forties, he found himself thinking more and more about those days. Today he had relived them. That was something special, and he savored the experience, knowing that as the years passed and he got older and older, the chance to relive his youth would come less and less—until it came not at all.

When Berg thought about his time in Vietnam, as he did that afternoon, his emotions were never clear-cut. He wasn't troubled by post traumatic stress, even though he had been under fire plenty of times, but he wondered how close he had come to having his mind wounded beyond repair. Whenever he thought about his good times in the Army, the bad times crept up on him, especially those during the three months he escorted convoys in and out of Bien-Hoa seven days a week in an MP Jeep with the seats and floor piled high with flack jackets, waiting every minute for a landmine to go off or for the Viet Cong to spring an ambush. Worrying about mines was bad, Berg remembered, but not as bad as waiting for the ambush he knew would hit some part of the convoy as it wove its way through the jungle.

Maybe it was because he had liked his MP duty in Saigon, where he spent nine months of his tour, that his thoughts about Vietnam mostly were pleasant. He had been shot at in Saigon, but somehow the terror hadn't come to him there as it had on convoys.

As he turned the Corvette onto his street, Berg's thoughts turned to Willard lying on the stairs. There was something about

Larry Soderquist

Willard's labcoat that knocked about in Berg's brain, and he wondered what it was. Berg's wife was a biologist, so he was used to seeing labcoats. But it wasn't just labcoats he had on his mind, it was labcoats and bodies. Then he remembered a poem by an anatomy professor. It ended,

> Day by night and night by day
> These bodies tug at my labcoat and whisper,
> "Live."

Chapter Two

OVER THE WEEKEND, BERG FOUND HIMSELF STRANGELY MOVED BY THE EVENTS OF Friday. He worked the facts of Willard's death over in his mind with detachment, the kind of cold and unaffected detachment shared by murder squad detectives and coroners, most of whom could eat a bag lunch surrounded by open guts and severed limbs. But when he wasn't thinking directly about the facts, he found that he couldn't be detached from them, for they saddened him. Perhaps it was the image of a body wrapped in a labcoat that got to him. In any case, he couldn't stop thinking about himself and his wife Eve or about heart attacks and the other ailments of middle age he feared were creeping closer to each of them.

But thinking about Willard's death also invigorated him, and that might have frightened him if he hadn't had the same experience many times before. He had learned in Vietnam that you never feel as alive as when a bullet has come close, but missed. Thinking about Willard's death reminded him that he, his wife, his two sons, and others that he loved were alive.

AFTER BREAKFAST ON MONDAY, BERG DECIDED TO TAKE GINGER, HIS German shepherd, for a walk, or rather Ginger took him. There was a long-abandoned farm behind the house, and as soon as Berg let Ginger out, that was where she headed. Mist from a heavy dampness in the air clung to the ground. The newly-risen sun's slanting rays pierced the mist, making it shimmer and causing the reddish blue of the morning sky to blend with the autumn browns of the low, treed hills ringing the old farm.

Over the next twenty minutes, Berg walked a mile and Ginger ran two or three, with all her casting about and cutting back. German shepherds weren't hunting dogs, but Ginger didn't seem to care what other dogs might think if they saw her chasing rabbits. There were lots of rabbits in the fields, and this morning she found one to chase, through thickets and over old fences. Berg stood and watched, smiling, his jacket collar turned up against the dampness of the cool breeze that had started to blow.

Besides the rabbits, Ginger also liked the fields because of the grown-over patch of black raspberry bushes she had found there. When they were in season, Berg picked berries off the top of the bushes while Ginger ate from the bottom. That German shepherds didn't usually like fruit didn't seem to bother Ginger any more than did her predilection for running after rabbits. Raspberry season had been over for months, though, so Ginger could only sniff at the raspberry bushes, looking as if she hoped some of the black fruit would magically appear.

The Labcoat

Walking with his dog through the fields that morning set Berg at peace, making him forget labcoats, heart attacks, and death.

ON HIS DRIVE TO SCHOOL, BERG STOPPED AT THE PHOTO SHOP FOR THE pictures from the stairwell. He quickly shuffled through the images, checking to see if any needed to be reprinted. The colors in Berg's pictures weren't quite right, but then, he reflected, colors rarely were in modern prints, what with computers making all the decisions. Berg decided that the prints were good enough, and he charged them to the university police account and headed for his office.

"Hello, Irene," Berg began, as he walked into his secretary's room. "Did you hear about the professor who died in the chemistry building on Friday?"

"Sure," she said, after looking up from the computer screen in front of her. "I saw it on the news."

"Call the medical examiner's office, will you, and confirm it was a heart attack? I need it for the report. His name was Frank Willard."

Berg flipped on the lights in his office, sank into the thick seat of his desk chair, and started reading another professor's article on the interpretation of some difficult passages in Isaiah. Soon Irene put her head through the doorway.

"The M.E.'s office says they don't know anything about Frank Willard."

Berg wasn't surprised. "The clerk probably hasn't gotten the autopsy report yet. Find out when we should call back."

"I had her check. She says Willard's body hasn't been logged in. She checked for Friday and the weekend."

"Here we go again," Berg said, shaking his head and raising his arms in mock despair. "The body's probably still at the hospital. You'd better call and see what the foul-up is."

This time, sitting with his chair in his favorite leaned-back position, his feet on the corner of his desk, Berg got a couple of pages read. He could hear bits and pieces of what Irene was saying. He couldn't make it all out, but it registered that she had to hold while somebody looked for information, and then she was transferred to another somebody so she could start over again.

"You're not going to believe it," she said from the doorway, holding a notepad. "Turns out a resident in the emergency room released the body Friday night to the Moore & Kennely Funeral Home."

Berg knew he had to put aside the article on Isaiah and try to straighten out the mess. The M.E. hated loose ends, and if Willard's body were buried before the M.E.'s office got a look at it, he knew his department would get blamed, whether it was their fault or not. He set his feet back on the floor and dialed the M.E.'s number.

"Is Dr. Webster there?"

"He's in a meeting."

"What about Dr. Hillman?"

"They're both in the same meeting."

"This is Assistant Chief Berg at the University Police Department. Break in, will you? There's a body you'll want to see that may be about to be buried."

After shrugging his shoulders in Irene's direction, Berg held the handset to his ear and listened to himself breathe while he doodled on a note pad. Finally Berg heard Samuel Webster, the assistant county medical examiner, come on the line.

Webster was a big, outgoing man of about thirty-five whom Berg had met a year before. He didn't fit Berg's idea of a pathologist. He thought a pathologist should be an introvert. And small and pale.

"Eric, what's this about a body about to be buried?"

Berg filled Webster in on what he knew, and Webster said he would get Willard's body transferred to the county morgue and call Berg when he could close the Willard file.

"I'll be interested to hear what you find out about the foul-up," Berg said. "I suppose I should have expected it."

After Berg hung up the telephone, his research assistant, Jane Samuels, came in to check on his progress on the articles she'd found for him. Like most of Berg's research assistants over the years, she had been chosen mostly on her grades. But besides being bright and hard working, which jumped at him from her academic file, Jane was practical minded. That was important too but never showed up in a student's grades.

Jane was also strikingly beautiful, with long black hair and a soft clear complexion, along with a model's face and a body that Berg expected drove her male classmates crazy. Plus she had a sparkling smile that he was sure no one could resist.

Jane's smile, and the rest of her too, distracted him, and while he was glad to have her near him, he never understood why some men sought out beautiful women to work with, tempting themselves daily with impulses they couldn't give in to. And Berg's impulses got rolling when Jane was around.

Before long, Webster called back. "I've got the story for you," he began, "but your report isn't going to read too well. The body's been cremated."

"Good show," Berg said, frowning as he held up his index finger to tell Jane that he wouldn't be long. "How did that happen?"

"That's what I asked the resident in the emergency room who signed the release. He says Willard's wife came to the ER after he had checked the body and decided it looked like Willard had died of a heart attack. The wife told him Willard had a bad heart and gave him the name of Willard's doctor. The resident made a quick call to the other doctor, who confirmed the bad heart—heart attack a couple of years ago. Willard's doctor also said Willard was forty pounds overweight and refused to go on a diet. With that, the resident signed the death certificate, listing cardiac arrest as the cause of death."

Berg had held his temper so far, though it was hard for him to do when the sloppiness of others caused him problems. Since he was a perfectionist himself, he expected the same of others. While listening to Webster, he found his temper rising. "What about the police hold?" he said, with an edge on his voice.

"There wasn't any. That's what the resident told me, and I confirmed it with the detective bureau. Friday was a busy afternoon, and their sergeant got tied up on other things and forgot to call."

"You'd think the resident would have wondered why there wasn't a hold, or at least would have looked for some indication in the paperwork that the police had released the body."

"Maybe, but in the guy's defense, he was busy too, with an ER full of live people," Webster said. "Actually," Webster went on, "what he did made pretty good sense. Anyway, Willard's wife called the funeral people and had the body picked up. She told them she wanted it cremated as soon as possible. So they kept the body overnight and had it cremated Saturday morning."

"So what do we do?" Berg asked, putting his anger aside and accepting the fact that he was going to have to do some extra work.

"I hate to tell you, but in a death like this one, state law says that either the M.E.'s office has to check the body or there has to be a complete police investigation. And you know the M.E.'s love for clean paperwork."

"I've heard," Berg said, pulling up the corners of his mouth as he always did when forced to accept something he didn't like.

"You can let the city police worry about it," Webster suggested.

"Sure, but they'd control the paperwork, and then it's my department that would take the blame—which would get back to my chief. He isn't happy when we look like clowns."

"I'm sure that's true," Webster said, smiling to himself, seemingly at the reminder that he wasn't the only one who had to live daily with bureaucratic infighting.

"So tell me, Dr. Watson," Berg began in a lighter vein, doing a poor imitation of how he assumed Sherlock Holmes would have sounded, "what does a 'complete police investigation' mean to the M.E.?"

"Funny you should ask, Mr. Holmes," playing the game but not trying to sound British. "I've heard the M.E. speak on that very subject. He wants what he calls clear and convincing evidence of the cause of death. Here we've got evidence of a heart attack, so nothing has to be done on the medical side. As a practical matter, what the police have to do is rule out homicide."

"And if we don't?"

"Then, besides the M.E. getting into a tiff, he'll change the cause of death on the death certificate to 'undetermined.' One problem there is the family's peace of mind. Also, life insurance companies may refuse to pay a claim until the beneficiary wins a lawsuit against them."

"What about the current death certificate?" Berg asked, knowing it already was in the process somewhere.

"We just called the county clerk's office and told them to send the paperwork to us, so there won't be a death certificate until we either let the current version go or issue a new one. That by itself will hold up any property transfers or life insurance payments, which is too bad, because this sure sounds like a simple heart attack to me."

"Me too," said Berg resignedly.

"There is one thing, though," Webster said after what to Berg seemed a moment's reflection. "The widow does appear to be remarkably efficient."

Up to this point Berg had assumed everything to be the result of a mix-up, but if he were going to do an investigation he knew he'd have to start thinking differently, thinking suspiciously. Thought of in that light, Mrs. Willard's actions were odd. When he was a pastor, he never ran into any widows who rushed to see how quickly they could get their husband's bodies turned into ashes.

"So, what else besides a heart attack could Willard have died from?" Berg asked, trying to find some place to start an investigation.

"Besides a couple of other natural causes, a quick acting poison could have done it. You found the body in a stairwell?"

"Yeah, that's right, and he was carrying an armload of books."

"Well, that doesn't sound much like quick-acting poison."

"Agreed," Berg said. Then, playing the devil's advocate, he asked, "But what about timed-release capsules or something? Couldn't someone have poisoned him that way?"

"I suppose. Or maybe his wife hired a Marilyn Monroe look-alike with a fifty-inch chest to flash him on the stairs wearing nothing but nylons and a garter belt. Probably would have keeled him right over, leaving no trace but a smile on his face."

"Very funny," Berg said, trying to sound sarcastic, but laughing as he thought about the woman opening a raincoat and wiggling a little bit, and Willard gasping and falling, clutching his books.

"What I'm saying is, there are all sorts of weird possibilities, but none of them is likely. You should think about something I learned in medical school: 'When you hear hoofbeats, think horses, not zebras.' Most likely what you've got here is a plain, ordinary heart attack."

Chapter Three

AT A QUARTER TO TWELVE, BERG DECIDED TO GIVE UP STUDYING ISAIAH. HE HAD tried to get his mind back to reading, but after his last conversation with Webster, he couldn't do it. He imagined that Webster was right. Willard most likely had died of a heart attack. But since he now had to do an investigation, doubts kept sneaking up on him, and he couldn't concentrate on anything else but Willard's death. He threw the article he had been trying to read on his desk and headed out his door.

"I'm going to the faculty club for lunch, Irene. I'll be back in about an hour."

The club was on the south edge of the campus in what had been a fashionable turn-of-the-century house. It was brick, two-storied Georgian, and handsome. Inside, most of the smaller rooms, which Berg expected had once served as bedrooms for the large family typical of the times, had been combined by knocking out walls. Nevertheless, the club retained a coziness from having several separate dining rooms, almost all with fireplaces that once had given the house its only heat.

Most of the rooms in the club had tables for four or six. In one room there were three tables set for eight, for people who wanted to take a chance on their dining companions. Although any member of the faculty was welcome there, the room tended to be the on-and-off gathering place of the same fifty or so people. It was to that room, the first on the right at the top of the stairs, that Berg went.

"So, Eric, I haven't seen you in awhile. Caught any bad guys lately?"

Berg smiled at Bill Clancy, a regular from the business school who, he had heard, was one of the country's great experts in statistics. Berg hadn't gone beyond high school geometry, and he knew that he would be lost if a conversation with Clancy ever turned to statistics.

"No such luck," Berg replied as he pulled the white linen napkin out of a water glass and put it on his lap.

"What was the commotion in the chemistry department on Friday?" one of the other regulars asked, looking at Berg. "I saw a police car and an ambulance there for a long time."

"One of the professors collapsed in the stairwell. Frank Willard. Anybody know him?"

"We were in the same department," Jerry Duncan said. "A nice guy."

"I knew him too," Clancy said. "What happened to him?"

"Heart attack most likely." But as Berg answered, he felt a little twinge of unease, like somebody was trying to tell him what he had said was wrong. That sensation always made Berg think about the guardian angel he believed he had, but wasn't sure about. Berg often wished his angel would come through a little clearer if the angel were there.

"Somebody fouled up and let the body be cremated before the coroner could see it," Berg continued, "so we may never know for sure. The coroner has a good idea of what could have happened though." Berg smiled and repeated Webster's surmise about the Marilyn Monroe look-alike on the stairs. "Bill," he said, "you're the statistician. What's the chance Willard went like that?"

"Beats me," Clancy said. "I'd have to do some research. If you see a woman like that walking around the campus, send her over and I'll get started on it."

Lunch went on for another half-hour, with nothing more intellectual than that getting discussed. In fact, it seemed to Berg that there was an unspoken rule that nothing intellectual ever got talked about at lunch—probably, Berg thought, the group's way of keeping lunch from being ruined by an "I'm smarter than you" competition.

As Berg was finishing eating the cheesecake he had tried and been unable to resist, Jerry Duncan came over and said in a low voice that he wanted some advice.

"I've been thinking about getting a handgun," Duncan began. "I've looked at different ones, and I don't know what to get."

"Do you want a carry permit?"

"No, I just want to keep the gun in the house."

"Do you have any kids at home?" Berg asked.

"No, I live alone."

"Where did you get the idea you want a handgun?"

"I don't know. There have been burglaries in the neighborhood. I just thought I'd feel better if I had something to defend the house with."

"I can understand that," Berg said. "But why a handgun?"

"I don't know. I don't know anything about guns. I just thought that's what the police use."

"Only if they don't have any other choice. The police carry pistols in holsters, but they keep shotguns in their cars."

"You think that's what I need?"

"If you want to get a gun to keep in the house, a shotgun would be a lot better than a handgun. Easier to use, more likely to connect with what you're shooting at, more power. And a shotgun is sure scarier to look down the barrel of if you're a burglar."

ON THE DRIVE BACK TO HIS OFFICE, BERG STARTED THINKING AGAIN about Willard. He wondered, seriously this time, what the odds were that Willard didn't die of a heart attack, and he had no idea. If he had been a big city homicide detective, with more bodies to wade over than time to worry about, he probably would have stopped wondering about Willard and let the M.E. do what he pleased about the incomplete report, including raise hell with the chief of police. But he did have time, so he wondered. Before he got his car parked, he came up with one idea.

Back in his office, he sat at his desk and dialed Sam Webster. "Sam, this is Eric. Let me ask you another question. How reasonable would it be to expect traces of poison, if that's what got him, to be on Willard's clothes?"

"Could happen," Webster answered, drawing his words out as if thinking while he was speaking. "It's not unusual for a poison victim to drool. Or I suppose he could wipe a sleeve across his mouth. What the chances are, I can't tell you."

Berg pondered for a second. "I'll do a little checking. If I find anything, I'll let you know. By the way, what's the name of the resident who signed the death certificate?"

"Let me see," Webster said, rummaging around on his desk for his notes. "Here it is, Arnold Hershey. University extension 3-2157."

Berg wrote the name and number on a note pad. He figured he might as well start his investigation where Willard's body began its journey to ashes. He dialed Hershey's number.

"Hello. Emergency room, nurses' station."

"Dr. Hershey please. It's the university police." Berg was put on hold, but at least he could wait in silence. Evidently the hospital thought that people calling the emergency room nurses' station wouldn't want to hear music while they waited. Everyone else in town plugged waiting callers into WYEZ, the local easy listening station.

As Hershey came on the line, Berg wondered if he ever left the emergency room. But any sympathy he might have felt for Hershey because of his long hours quickly departed.

"This is Dr. Hershey."

"Hello," Berg began. "This is Assistant Chief Berg of the university police. I'm calling about Frank Willard, who was brought to the ER late Friday afternoon."

"I know. Don't you guys ever stop? Someone already called here this morning, and then the M.E.'s office called again."

"Well, I'm sorry to bother you, but there are some things I need to know. How'd it happen that you released the body?"

Berg could feel an attempt at a brush-off coming.

"I don't have time for this," Hershey said. "You'll have to ask the M.E.'s office."

Like most cops, Berg knew to stay on the good side of ER people. Partly because police often had business in the emergency room, and being friendly helped ease things along. But also because they knew that they might be brought into the hospital on a cart themselves, and they wanted friends to work on them. When pushed, however, Berg's temper overrode practicalities, especially when he, a full professor, was talking to a resident in training.

"Don't screw with me, you piss-ant," Berg warned through clenched teeth. "Who do you think you're talking to?" Then, without waiting for an answer, he bullied ahead. "Unless you've got somebody dying over there, you'll talk to me now. Either on the phone or I'll come and haul your ass to the University Police Station—and that's before I tell the chief of medicine that you're an idiot. I'm trying to forget that you released a body without approval, which has now been cremated, causing me no end of trouble."

Hershey apparently decided he'd better talk then. "Look, that wasn't my fault," he began, his earlier arrogance now seemingly replaced with anxiety. "There was every reason to believe that Frank

Willard died of a heart attack, and no one told me the police were involved. I examined the body and talked to his personal physician—who, by the way, is one of the top cardiologists around."

"Okay, okay. What I really want to know is, how is it that you sent his body on its way to the crematorium."

"Mrs. Willard showed up maybe a half hour after the body got here. She told me about her husband's bad heart and wanted me to call his doctor."

"How'd his wife know to come to your ER?" Berg asked.

Hershey paused, then said, "I'm sure we didn't call her because we hadn't had time to process the body in yet. All I'd done by then was take a quick look at it. I guess I thought the police called her."

Berg knew that hadn't happened. He had expected the emergency room to call, which was the standard procedure. They would have called in Willard's case, Berg was sure, if Willard's wife hadn't showed up on her own.

Here was another mystery for Berg to solve, but this one meant the case was getting more interesting.

"How'd she seem?"

"I don't know. She seemed like her husband had just died," Hershey answered, sounding to Berg like he was above being bothered by the question.

"Distraught, frantic, nervous, what?" Berg pushed, his tone and the force of his voice indicating that he hadn't liked the apparent change in Hershey's attitude.

"Well, a little of all those, I guess," Hershey said, again polite. "Those things all look pretty much alike."

"Let's talk about nervous," Berg said.

"Yeah, I'd say she was nervous. But people act all types of ways around here."

It was clear now that Berg was going to have to talk to Willard's nervous but efficient widow. He told Hershey that was all for the time being and hung up.

"Irene, call that funeral home and see if you can get the manager on the phone, will you please?"

While he waited, Berg jotted down on his note pad some questions he wanted answered.

The Labcoat

"The funeral director is on the line. His name's Herman Krimmer."

Berg picked up. "Hello, Mr. Krimmer. This is Assistant Chief Berg of the university police. I'm calling about the body you had cremated Saturday."

"Yes, Dr. Webster called this morning. I'm sorry about the mess. We try to do things properly, but everything looked in order," Krimmer said, sounding concerned.

"I know. Nobody's blaming you. You can help me with a few things, though. Tell me about the wife. How did she seem to you? Did she seem nervous?"

"No, I'd say she seemed matter-of-fact."

"Isn't that strange?" Berg asked, turning his head slightly as he held the phone.

"No, I wouldn't say so. Nothing is strange in this business. Some cry, some laugh. You never know what you'll see. Grief comes out in strange ways."

That's just about what the resident said, Berg thought to himself. And he remembered the same thing from his days as a pastor, so he realized his questions weren't getting him anywhere. He decided to try a different direction. "What percentage of people want cremations?"

"Oh, maybe 20 percent. Nothing really unusual about that. It's even more for university people."

"Do you usually have people who are interested in how quickly you will get a cremation done?"

"No," Krimmer said. Then after a short wait he continued, "I'd say that is unusual. I really didn't think too much about it at the time, though. Mrs. Willard said she didn't like to think of her husband's body lying on a slab."

Berg figured he had gotten about as much as he could from Krimmer on that subject, so he turned to Willard's clothes. "You still have the clothes Willard was wearing?"

"No. I asked Mrs. Willard if she wanted to keep them, but she said no. It makes a difference how we handle them. The easiest way is to cut them off, so that's what we did."

"Even his shoes?" Berg asked, before deciding too late that it was a silly question.

"Not the shoes. We don't cut those off, but we don't keep them either, unless the client wants them."

"Client?" Berg thought. He had wondered what funeral directors call the people who pay their bills. "Customer" sounded cold, but "client" didn't seem quite right either. Berg hoped that he'd find that the funeral home's trash hadn't been picked up yet, so Willard's clothes could be retrieved, but no such luck. Krimmer said it had been collected early that morning.

"So, is not wanting a husband's clothes unusual?" Berg asked, struggling for some way to get a handle on Willard's wife.

"Unless he died wearing a new suit that she'd want to give away, they usually don't want the clothes. Actually, when we ask them about the clothes, I guess that's the first time most of them think about all the stuff of their husband's that they're going to have to deal with, and they usually take the chance to cross one thing off their list."

"Okay," Berg said, taking his last shot. "What do you have of Willard's?"

"Well, let me see. Hold the phone a second."

While he waited, Berg doodled on his note pad. He drew little pairs of shoes, evidently because that was what he had on his mind.

Krimmer came back on the line. "Here it is," he said. Then he recited carefully, "Wallet, watch, wedding ring, keys, comb, reading glasses, some change, and his labcoat."

On hearing the last item, Berg's mood brightened and he sat up straight. "Why didn't you toss the labcoat too?" Berg asked.

"It says on it that it's university property, plus it has a radiation safety badge on the pocket—what they use to keep track of radiation you've been exposed to. I thought the university would want it back."

"Good thinking," Berg said. "Keep all that stuff until I get over there. If the widow shows up, tell her there's a police hold on it. Also, if that does happen, pay attention to how she acts. Is she aggravated, scared, or what?"

"Okay," Krimmer said, dragging out the word and sounding uncertain. Probably didn't like the idea of playing cop with a client, Berg thought.

Chapter Four

NOW THAT HE HAD FINALLY CAUGHT A BREAK, BERG DECIDED TO PURSUE IT RIGHT then, even though he should have been preparing to teach his three o'clock class on the theology of the early church. Berg wan't concerned about the class, though, because he'd found that he usually taught best the classes he prepared for the least. He knew there was a lesson for him in that, although he had trouble deciding just what it was.

"I'm going over to that funeral home," he told his secretary, "but I'll be back before class."

On the drive over, he wondered if he was just wasting time. He believed Webster was right. He was searching for a zebra when what he had was a horse. But Berg was an absolutist. Either he pursued something full out or he didn't fool with it at all.

He parked his car along the side of the Moore & Kennely Funeral Home and walked through the awning-covered front door of the gray clapboard building. He was met immediately.

"Good afternoon. May I help you, sir?"

"I need to see Mr. Krimmer. I'm Eric Berg."

"Yes, Mr. Berg, I'm Herman Krimmer," the man said, extending his right hand to Berg. "Let's go back to my office."

As Berg followed Krimmer down a hallway and into a comfortable office decorated in American traditional, he took a measure of the funeral director. Krimmer fit the image. Dark gray suit, white broadcloth shirt, plain gold cufflinks, dark red tie with a small blue paisley print, plain black shoes. Krimmer didn't wear a white carnation, but he looked like he should have. Or maybe, Berg thought, he was just being affected by the surroundings. Krimmer was about fifty and his face wore a how-can-I-help-you expression.

"I have Mr. Willard's things right here for you," Krimmer said as he motioned Berg to a sofa behind a coffee table, on which Berg saw what Krimmer had described on the telephone.

Berg sat down, picked up the wallet, and started going through it. Still fifty-four dollars here, he thought to himself, noting that Krimmer had proven himself to be honest—or at least honest in small things, which he knew was not the same as honest. He found nothing of interest. Driver's license, university I.D., MasterCard, membership cards in a couple of scientific societies, and an emergency identification card naming his wife, Doris Willard, as the contact person.

Berg had hoped for something like a list of interesting phone numbers. He picked up the key ring. Two keys he recognized as coming from the university, probably one for the chemistry building and one for Willard's office. Also, there were keys for a Ford and a G.M. car, a house key, and a smaller key that Berg hoped was to Willard's desk.

From his army days, Berg knew that someone always went through the belongings of dead soldiers and removed anything that might cause pain to relatives. Usually that meant condoms or some other evidence of infidelity if the soldier was married. A number of times, he had been there when a dead soldier's belongings were packed. If no one else had removed such things, he had done it. Berg wondered if funeral directors did that too. He assumed so.

"Did you throw anything out? Say something his wife maybe shouldn't see?" Berg asked.

Krimmer looked surprised at the question, and then sheepish. "No," he said, "there was nothing like that." He didn't seem to think that Berg was satisfied, so he added, "We do remove things like that, but what you see here is all there was."

Berg nodded and began gathering up the items he had looked through, along with the labcoat. "I'd like to take these along," he told Krimmer, motioning to the other items. "I'll give them to Mrs. Willard personally."

"I knew you wanted the labcoat, but I don't know about the other things. I really ought to have them here for her. Her husband's ashes are ready, and she may be by any time."

"The problem is," Berg said firmly, standing up at the same time, "they're part of a police investigation, and I have to take custody of them. I'll give you a receipt, and you can show it to Willard's wife if she asks. Here, give me a piece of paper."

Like most people confronted with authority, especially if given an easy out, Krimmer acquiesced. He found a blank piece of paper and waited while Berg wrote out a receipt, listing each item, including fifty-four dollars and seventy-eight cents in cash. Then Krimmer found a paper bag for Willard's belongings, and Berg left. As he did, he noticed that Krimmer still didn't look like he wanted to tell Doris Willard that the police had her husband's things.

On his way back to the divinity school, Berg was confronted by the dichotomy between what he knew the police were supposed to do and what he did himself. He had to face the fact that although he believed that laws and rules ought to be obeyed, he didn't always follow them. The day isn't over yet, Berg thought, and I've bullied an ER doctor by a threat to haul him in without any authority, and I've conned a funeral director out of a dead man's belongings with no right, because I wanted to lie to his widow about why I was visiting her.

Berg guessed that he thought about such things because he was a divinity school professor, and he noticed that he was more interested in his thoughts than concerned by them. Maybe he should feel otherwise, he decided, but all he felt was satisfaction that he had gotten something done.

After teaching his class, Berg left school for the last time that day. He had decided that before going home, he would drive the twenty miles to the state police central crime laboratory and drop off Willard's labcoat.

Because of his position, Berg sometimes went to meetings with ranking people in departments around the state, and he had met the state police laboratory's director a year ago at a meeting about how the police might talk the legislature into buying the extraordinarily expensive equipment required to do DNA fingerprinting. It turned out that neither Berg nor anyone else could convince the legislature, so the police still had to use the FBI lab and wait for months, or use private labs that were not only backlogged, but expensive.

Berg asked to see the director, and after a couple of minutes a tall, gangly woman of about sixty came out to greet him. It appeared to Berg that she had bought her outfit, a floral print skirt and a baggy coat that was a size too large, from the Salvation Army. But he wasn't surprised. He had known from the first time he met her that she was interested in forensics, not clothes. "Hi, Eric," she said, putting out her hand. "Good to see you."

"Good to see you too, Molly," Berg said with affection as they shook hands. He then laid the bag he carried on a desk and continued, "I've got a labcoat here that one of our chemistry professors had on when he died. There was a foul-up and the body got cremated before the M.E. could see it. This is all that's left, and I hoped you could check for traces of a quick-acting poison that he may have gotten on it from his mouth. Maybe the left sleeve. When he died, he was on a stairway, and his body slipped down a couple of steps while he held onto some books that ended up above his head. I thought his sleeve may have rubbed past his mouth as the body went down."

"Sure, we can check that. Leave it here and I'll get a technician right on it. We should be able to call you tomorrow morning."

"Great," Berg said, smiling. "I never expected that kind of service."

"We like to take care of our friends. I appreciated the work you did with the legislature last year trying to get us the DNA equipment."

"Sorry it didn't work, but I was glad to try."

"That's what counts," Molly said as she picked up the bag. "We'll call you tomorrow."

Chapter Five

WHENEVER BERG WAS BUSY WORKING ON A COMPLICATED ARGUMENT FOR A BOOK OR an article in an academic journal, he did his best thinking while pacing back and forth in his office. His focus would be drawn down to a fine point and kept precisely aimed. But his morning walks with Ginger were his best times for reflection. On those walks, he let his mind wander wherever it would. He had found that when he relaxed and turned his mind loose, he had insights he never would have had by shoving and pushing it down a narrow corridor.

As Berg watched Ginger run through the fields and jump fences the next morning, his mind worked over many things. The air was clear and dry, and the sun strong, so everything he saw with his eyes, he saw crisply.

Ginger scared up a pheasant, and as it flew away, squawking, Berg could make out the subtle shadings of browns and oranges in its plumage until it flew between him and the sun and disappeared into the brightness of the sun's rays.

The things that he saw in his mind that morning, he didn't see clearly. He kept going over the question of good and evil, or rather his relationship to good and evil. He asked himself what he wanted the state police laboratory to find on Willard's labcoat. Did he want them to find poison, which probably meant that Willard had been murdered? It didn't take him long to answer that question. He knew that he did want that, and he wondered what that meant for him.

Berg told himself he merely wanted to be the one to discover a murder, and to find the murderer, because that would make his life more interesting, more exciting. But he knew he couldn't let himself off that easily, because for him to find the murderer, there had to have been a murder, and he knew he wished that to be.

ONCE IN HIS OFFICE, THE MORNING PROVIDED HIM ONLY AN HOUR OF reading before the state police laboratory called.

"Chief Berg," the lab technician began, "this is John Bleicher. I've just finished the tests on the labcoat you brought in yesterday."

From his ruminations that morning, Berg knew how he wanted the tests to come out, but until the call came in, he hadn't been sure how much he wanted it. As he listened to the technician, he could sense tension gathering itself into a ball he felt in his stomach. "Great," Berg replied. "What did you find?"

"Just what you told Molly you wanted us to look for. Poison."

Berg felt a little internal leap of excitement as his body responded to the news. But he also felt something besides excitement. What was it? Shame, he realized. Shame because he had willed the murder to be and, what would prove to be more important, he had willed the existence of a murderer.

"I tried the inside of the left sleeve," the technician continued. "Near the end, where your victim may have rubbed it across his mouth. But there wasn't anything there."

As Bleicher talked, Berg thought about the fact that he had used the word *victim*. He wondered if finding poison meant to Bleicher that Willard had been murdered, or if he was just used to thinking of the artifacts he examined as coming from victims.

"Then I tried higher up on the sleeve in three or four places," Bleicher said. "When I got to a spot near the shoulder, I found the first trace of cyanide. That seemed like a strange place to find it, so I started trying other spots all over the labcoat, front, back, top, bottom. Here's what it comes down to. You've got traces of cyanide all over the top of the labcoat on the front. None on the back, sides, or bottom of the front."

Berg couldn't see how that fit with Willard drooling or rubbing his mouth on the coat, and said so.

"You're right," Bleicher said. "The incidence is too widespread, and also too even. I'll tell you something else, the traces are on the surface. The labcoat wasn't saturated anyplace so far as I could tell."

"What do you make of it?" Berg said.

"Only one thing I can think of. The top front of the coat was exposed to a vapor or fine spray of cyanide."

"How in the world would that have happened? Was the guy murdered, or what?"

"I don't know," the technician responded. "I also asked Molly, who's seen about everything. She doesn't know what to make of it either. The guy was a chemist, though, right?"

"Yes."

"If I were you, I'd check out his lab to see if he could have picked up the traces there. He may not have been exposed to enough cyanide to do him any harm, especially if he didn't get the exposure all at once."

"Good idea," Berg said. That made sense, but the prospect disappointed and relieved him at the same time. "I really appreciate your help," he went on. "Put the coat in an evidence bag and ship it back to me, will you? You can just send me your report along with it."

"I'll do it," Bleicher said. "Let us know what you find. This is a strange one."

After he put down the phone, Berg sat at his desk, trying to put aside his feelings while he figured out how to check out Willard's lab. Obviously he needed the help of someone who knew the way around the chemistry department. He didn't know the chair of the department, but decided to call anyway. That at least was a place to start. He grabbed the university telephone directory, which was the size of a directory for a small city, and found the number for the department. It didn't list who the chair was.

"Hello," Berg started when the secretary answered. "This is Eric Berg. I'm a professor at the Divinity School. I need to speak to the chair, but I've forgotten who that is now."

"James Lerner. Let me see if I can get him for you."

In less than a minute, Lerner came on the line.

"What can I do for you, Professor Berg?" Lerner said.

"I'd like to come and see you. Actually, I want to see you in my capacity as assistant chief of the university police. It's in connection with Frank Willard's death. I just didn't want to announce that. How would right after lunch be, say about one o'clock?"

Berg and Lerner agreed on the time, and Berg went back to reading the article on Isaiah, but again he had trouble concentrating. That wasn't too surprising, he thought. This was the first possible murder he had worked on since Saigon.

Chapter Six

At just a few minutes before one o'clock, Berg drove into the parking lot by the chemistry building and found an empty spot under an old oak tree. Its limbs were bare, but they themselves, gnarled and twisted together as they were, provided shade. He always tried to leave his car in the shade. Even in the fall, the sun's rays were powerful enough to make the inside of his glass-topped Corvette feel like Phoenix in July.

As he walked toward the building, Berg fell in behind two undergraduates, either of whom, from what he could see, could be Sam Webster's Marilyn Monroe look-alike. He found himself wanting to see what they looked like from the front, and as he went up the steps of the chemistry building after them, he hoped they might turn around when one of them opened the door. But somebody coming out opened the door for them, and they walked in with their backs toward him.

Berg punched the elevator button and rode to the sixth floor. After some searching, he found Lerner's office. So far as he could see, it was the only office on the floor that didn't open directly on the corridor. Since Lerner was the chair, he had a secretary sitting in an outer office running interference for him. Berg walked in and said who he was, but before the secretary could respond, Lerner came out of his office and took over.

"Come in, Professor Berg. Would you like some coffee?" Lerner was about Berg's size and in his mid-forties. His black hair, just starting to go a little white, gave him a distinguished air, as did the blue, pin-striped suit he wore. His suit and dark hair contrasted sharply with Berg's relaxed academic dress and Swedish-issue blond hair. Berg thought Lerner looked more like a banker than an academic.

Berg declined the coffee as he looked around Lerner's office. Swedes were supposed to drink coffee, and Berg's Swedish father had given him coffee when he was as young as he could remember. He guessed that was why he didn't like coffee any better than most people his age liked milk. He only drank it when he had to.

Lerner's office was sparse, furnished with an institutional gray metal desk and a couple of not-so-easy chairs, plus three file cabinets and a set of gray metal bookshelves. It was the style Berg recognized from the biology department, where his wife worked, as science department modern. He had concluded that since the science departments made up so much of the university's budget, they didn't want people in other departments to think they spent money on frivolities.

Berg wasn't much for the kind of preliminary small talk that characterized the beginning of most meetings, so he looked at Lerner and said simply, "I need to talk to you about Frank Willard's death, and for now I'd like you to keep our conversation to yourself."

Lerner seemed to appreciate getting down to business. "No problem," he said, smiling. "How can I help?"

"Let me tell you what we've found," Berg began. "The body was cremated before the medical examiner's office could look at it, but I had the state police crime lab check the labcoat Willard was wearing. They found traces of cyanide all over the front near the top, which they think was from a vapor or spray. What do you make of that?"

As Berg spoke, Lerner leaned forward and furrowed his forehead, making his eyes almost close. "I don't know what to make of it. It sounds scary. You think he was murdered?"

"I hoped you could help me answer that question," Berg countered. "What I need to know is, could he have been exposed to cyanide in his work?"

Berg expected a little reflection from Lerner, but he didn't get it. Lerner came back with a quick reply. "I don't see how."

"Why is that? He was a chemist. Who knows what he might have been working with?"

"You know the definition of a specialist. Someone who knows more and more about less and less. Willard was a specialist. Most people here are. He worked in one small branch of inorganic chemistry. It's not my area, but I know enough about it to say that there is no way he ever would have worked with cyanide."

"Could he have been helping someone else with an experiment?" Berg said.

"I suppose so, but I doubt it. Some people around here use cyanide from time to time, but I can't imagine why any of them would have needed Willard's help with it."

"Well, humor me. What if he did help someone? Could he have been exposed to a vapor or spray of the stuff?"

"He would have had to have been a pretty poor chemist to do that, and he wasn't. He was one of the best we have, a front runner, in fact, for the College of Science's prize for excellence in research." Lerner paused for a minute, then added, "Let's go into my lab. I want to show you something."

Berg followed Lerner two doors down the hall, into a large laboratory. In the center of the room, in two rows, were benches, with shelves of chemicals above. Lerner walked past the central benches to the back of the room.

"This," Lerner said, pointing, "is a fume hood." The contraption was a large metal cabinet that went from floor to ceiling along part of the lab's back wall. The lower portion had doors and appeared to be for storage. Above that was an enclosed workspace made of stainless steel. Berg saw that a large glass door could be pulled down in front. A technician, who Lerner introduced as the person who used most of the equipment in the lab, was mixing chemicals inside the hood. The glass door was pulled down so that it almost touched her arms. Berg could hear a blower and feel a draft as air from the room was drawn into the hood.

"Cyanide is very volatile stuff," Lerner explained. "No chemist would work with it outside a fume hood. With the glass door down most of the way and the hood sucking air up and out, vapors can't get into the room."

"Where do the vapors go?" Berg asked, mainly because he was curious.

"The exhaust from all the hoods in the building is collected near the roof and piped out a high stack, after it's run through a filter."

As they walked back to Lerner's office, Berg began to see more clearly that he likely had a murder on his hands, but he didn't know what he should do about it. All he could do for now, he thought, was follow the police doctrine he had been taught: in the absence of an obvious suspect, your best bets in a murder are spouses and the people who report finding bodies.

When he and Lerner were again in private, Berg started to pursue the first of the only two suspects he could think of. "How much do you know about Willard's wife?" he said to Lerner.

"I guess I've gotten to know her quite a bit over the years, by being together at dinner parties and so on. She'd stop by Frank's lab from time to time, so sometimes I'd run into her around the department."

"What kind of woman is she?"

"Nothing out of the ordinary. She's in her early forties, attractive. Likes to do things outside, plays tennis. Much different than Frank in those respects. She's never worked that I know of."

"Does she know anything about chemistry, as far as you can tell?"

"A little. I remember her telling me once that she'd been a premed student in college."

"Enough to know about how to deal with cyanide?" Berg said.

"Chemistry students are taught how to use fume hoods in a beginning course. Otherwise they'd kill themselves."

"Do you think of her as the nervous type?"

"No. Not at all."

"Would you say she is a decisive, take-charge kind of woman?" Berg said, trying to get an idea of whether her handling of the cremation was in character.

"I'd say she knows her own mind and isn't afraid to look out for her interests. She isn't any shrinking violet, if that's what you mean. And she's bright, probably as bright as Frank."

"She told the funeral director she wanted her husband's body cremated right away. Said she didn't want it left lying on a slab. He says it's unusual for a widow to push for a quick cremation. What do you think about that?"

Lerner thought a few seconds as he ran a hand through his black and white hair. "I'm a little surprised that she would be more concerned than most people about something like that, but it doesn't surprise me that she would tell a funeral director exactly what she wanted. That sounds like her."

"Let me ask you what may be a more important question," Berg continued, looking closely at Lerner so he could catch his reaction. "How did the Willards get along?"

"Fine, so far as I know. I never saw them gazing fondly into each other's eyes, but I never sensed any trouble."

"Did she have any affairs, as far as you know?"

"No," Lerner replied. "I've never heard anything like that. But I doubt that I would unless it got to be common knowledge around the department."

"What about Willard? Did he behave himself?"

Berg sensed that Lerner wasn't comfortable with the question. He seemed to draw back a little, and he avoided Berg's eyes as he answered. "I guess so. At least I don't know that he didn't."

Berg wasn't satisfied, so he asked more questions like the last one, but to no avail. Lerner wouldn't admit that he knew anything about Willard and other women. Perhaps he's been fooling around himself, Berg thought, and the questions were too close to home.

Berg changed his focus. "What can you tell me about the secretary who found the body? I've forgotten her name."

"Marilyn Harris," Lerner said. "She's worked here for a few years. Not the best secretary we've got, but she gets by."

"What about her and Willard?" Berg asked. "Any connection?"

"There was once. She was working on a manuscript for one of his books, and she somehow deleted several chapters from her computer. Turned out she'd never made a backup and said she couldn't find Willard's handwritten copy."

Berg thought about what he'd do if a secretary did that to one of his manuscripts. Wring her neck is what came to mind. "So what happened?" Berg said.

"Willard was so upset he couldn't bring himself to come to work for a week. Can't say I blame him—he lost a lot of hard work. He wanted Marilyn fired, but other professors stuck up for her, so she stayed."

"Who made that decision?"

"I did. It was damned if I did and damned if I didn't. What it came down to was numbers, I guess. I'd have made more people mad by firing her than by keeping her."

"What about Willard and her after that?"

"Oh, he wouldn't have anything to do with her. Would hardly speak to her even. Continued to complain about her, though. Every time secretaries were evaluated, he'd try again to get rid of her."

That Berg could understand. The more interesting issue was, how did Marilyn Harris react? Berg asked Lerner about that.

"Funny thing there. She appeared to stay above it all. In fact, that's one of the things that made Willard so mad at her. She never really seemed to understand how much damage she had done, and never seemed too concerned about what Willard thought of her either."

"What do you get from that?" Berg asked.

"I don't know. Sometimes I think she's dumb as a rock, and at other times she makes me believe she's as smart as anyone else around here—and that's saying something."

Lerner paused and pulled a piece of lint off his coat, looking pensive. Berg thought it best just to let quiet do its work. He'd found that if you wait long enough, most people will do almost anything to break an awkward silence.

"I don't know that I should say this," Lerner continued, "because it was just a feeling. But the first time I talked to her about the problem with Willard's manuscript, I thought I saw a Cheshire cat grin just beneath the surface—like she'd done it on purpose."

"Why would she do that?"

"I don't know," Lerner said. "There are some SOBs around here that any secretary might like to get back at, but Willard wasn't one of them. It never made sense to me."

Berg made a mental note that Marilyn Harris was going to have to be checked out along with Willard's widow, but he didn't think he was likely to learn much more from Lerner.

"We need to know if anyone in the building saw anybody in the stairwell or coming out of it at about the time Willard died, or saw anything at all unusual," Berg said. "Would you be willing to post some notices around the building asking anyone who saw anything like that to call me?"

"Sure, no problem. I'll get it done this afternoon."

"I appreciate that. Maybe you could take me by Willard's office. I have his keys and I'd like to look around."

"Sure, it's just down the hall."

Berg followed Lerner past his own laboratory and then to a cross-over hall that took them to the other side of the building. As they approached the end of the corridor near the stairwell, Lerner turned into a laboratory that had Willard's name on the door. It seemed to be a copy of the lab Lerner had shown him earlier, except that this one had an office tucked inside.

"This is it," Lerner said. "Things are pretty slow around his lab now," evidently referring to the fact that no one was there. "We're trying to decide what to do with his graduate students and technicians."

Berg took out Willard's keys and fitted one he recognized as a university key into the lock. That one didn't work, so he tried the other one and this time the door opened. Berg looked around for a moment, then realized that the books Willard had been carrying up the stairs were not there.

"What do you suppose happened to the books Willard had with him when he died?" Berg said. "Marilyn Harris was going to bring them to his office."

"I don't know. Her desk is just down the hall. I'll go ask her."

As Lerner left, Berg began his search of Willard's office. The office was small, less than half the size of Lerner's, but furnished with the same institutional furniture. Desk and chair, two side chairs, some bookshelves, and a locked file cabinet.

Berg started with the desk. Only the big drawer on the bottom right was locked. He looked through the other drawers first, hoping that Willard's scientific mind had been more orderly than his desk, because the drawers were a jumble. Berg had just finished going through the last unlocked drawer, having found nothing, when Lerner returned with Marilyn Harris.

"The policeman and I put the books right here," she said, pointing to an empty space in a bookcase in the lab near the office, which Berg could see from his place at Willard's desk.

"I thought you were going to put them in his office," Berg said as he got up and went toward the door.

"We were, but they were heavy and I saw the empty space on the shelf, so we put them there. I didn't think anyone cared where we put them."

"Don't worry about it," Berg told her with a casual wave of his hand, not wanting to put her on guard. "It's not important."

After she left, Berg asked Lerner to try to find out what happened to the books. Berg didn't explain further, but the only interesting possibility he could think of was that the books might have gotten the same dose of cyanide as the labcoat, and whoever was responsible could have taken them to destroy the evidence.

Marilyn Harris had made that a whole lot easier, Berg knew, by leaving the books on an open shelf. Also, he suspected that Tommy Allbright, the patrolman who had helped her, had not made her carry any of the load, since he was big enough to carry both her and the books if he had wanted to. So Berg doubted she would have given much thought to the weight of the books.

He thanked Lerner for his help, and when he was sure that Lerner had left the lab, began once again to look through Willard's office.

First he tried the key that looked like it was for a desk. The key fit Willard's bottom right drawer, and Berg turned the key in the lock and pulled the drawer open, wondering what he would find. Evidently Willard had been on a tenure committee because he had files on the tenure reviews of three assistant professors.

Berg also found a more interesting file. It had no label, but when he began to go through it, he saw that it was a catalogue of incidents involving Lerner. Some of the incidents related to the episode with Marilyn Harris, but that was a small part of the file.

The items in the file included Willard's notes and documents that Willard evidently thought proved derelictions against Lerner. Everything was in chronological order, and Berg found it particularly interesting that the first items referred to incidents involving Willard's wife before he had married her. It seemed that Willard and Lerner were unfriendly competitors for her affection.

Berg found that two themes ran through the file, Lerner's supposed unfair treatment of Willard and his misuse of federal grants. Many of the documents tied department spending from grants to items unrelated to the grants. It appeared to Berg that until about six months before, when things changed, Lerner had essentially been throwing money from several grants into one big slush fund and spending the money on whatever department project he wished. How Willard had used the file, or planned to, and whether Lerner knew of the file, Berg couldn't learn from the documents.

In the locked desk drawer Berg also found a key for the file cabinet. He opened the cabinet and spent a half hour going through it, looking for nothing in particular—just anything that might give someone a motive to kill, maybe Willard's widow or Marilyn Harris, or now it seemed, Lerner. He found nothing helpful.

The only reason for keeping the cabinet locked appeared to be that it contained a file of several years' letters from the university telling Willard what his salary would be for the next year. Berg was sure that Willard's colleagues would like to see that file, since salaries were one of the few kept secrets in a university. He didn't know exactly what to expect for chemistry professors' salaries, but he had some idea based on his wife's salary in the biology department. It looked like Willard had been well-paid.

Berg picked up the file on Lerner and then started to leave. He had shut off the light and was about to walk out the door when it struck him that he had left unchecked the best hiding place in the room—under the locked bottom desk drawer.

Berg sat down at Willard's desk and unlocked the drawer again. This time he pulled it all the way out of the desk and felt around. His hand hit upon one video tape and then another. Nothing else.

Berg slid the drawer back into the desk before looking at the tapes. Both were X-rated and showed two men with one woman. Berg had been inside his share of porno shops as an MP officer, but Willard's tapes looked raw compared to what he'd seen on the shelves. He reminded himself that his experience was more than a few years old, and that porno wasn't likely to have gotten softer in the meantime. He had no idea how the tapes might be relevant, but he found a large manila envelope in Willard's file cabinet and put them in to take along. He figured that, if nothing else, he would throw them out at some point, having at least saved Willard the posthumous embarrassment of someone else finding them.

After checking under the other bottom desk drawer, and finding nothing, Berg closed up Willard's lab and drove back to his office. He decided that he'd better call Sam Webster and fill him in on what he had learned. He got Webster on the phone and told him about the state police lab's findings and what he'd found from his visit to the chemistry department. He then asked one of the two questions that were on his mind.

"Do you want to change the records on Willard's cause of death?" Berg said.

"I don't think so, not now. But it depends a little on what you want to do."

"What do you mean?" Berg asked, not knowing what to expect.

"Well, we may or may not have enough evidence yet to call it murder. But, if we do and I make the change, it becomes a city police case. The problem is, they are going to be too busy to pursue a whodunit. I also doubt they could work around the university the way you can."

That seemed to answer the other question Berg had on his mind, which was whether this was still his case. "I'm willing to stay with it," Berg said. "I'll keep you informed."

However, being willing to stay with the investigation and knowing what to do with it were two different things. For the rest of the afternoon and through dinner at home with Eve, the question of where to go was on his mind.

He went through the possibilities with his wife, as he often did with things he was working on. It was obvious that Lerner and Marilyn Harris needed to be looked at. He was particularly troubled that Lerner had lied to him about how well he knew Willard's wife and how he'd come to know her, especially since Berg could see no reason why an innocent man would want to hide an old romantic rivalry. On the other hand, it was Lerner who had shown Berg the fume hood and tried to convince him that Willard couldn't have been exposed to cyanide by chance. But perhaps Lerner thought quickly enough to decide that openness was his safest bet, since Lerner would have no idea who else Berg might talk to about cyanide.

Then there was the idea of Willard and another woman, which would give Willard's wife a motive. He wasn't at all satisfied that Lerner had told him everything he knew on that subject, and the video tapes added to his suspicion. Since they were in Willard's office, he must have had someplace besides home to watch them.

Eve focused right away on the question of what Lerner might have been trying to hide about Willard and another woman, and she was the one who knew how to proceed.

"I've got a friend in the chemistry department, someone I know through the women's faculty group. I bet she'll know anything Lerner knows."

"And she'll tell you?"

"Sure she will. Why not? Women don't like to gossip any more than men, but they like to gossip just as much."

"All right, just tell her to keep her mouth shut," Berg warned.

"That shows how much you know about how to conduct an investigation. I'll just let on that I heard Willard might have been involved with another woman and see what she says. She's not likely to tell anyone I called if that's all I say."

Chapter Seven

BERG TAUGHT A CLASS ON ETHICS WEDNESDAY MORNING, WITH THE USE OF FORCE as the topic for the day. Home videos had put police brutality on television, and watching had made students think they were experts. Because he wanted his students to hear the police's side of the story, he talked a city police patrol sergeant into meeting with the class, along with an assistant DA. Berg listened along with his students.

"Why don't you arrest police when they run amuck?" a third-year student asked the DA. "They aren't any better than anyone else."

"We do in serious cases," the DA said. Berg could see that she was trying to find a way to distinguish serious police brutality from some other type, but was not finding it easy to do.

"What do you mean 'serious cases?' There's no excuse for excess force," the student countered. "There are laws against assault, and when the police use excess force, that's assault."

The patrol sergeant stepped in. "That works for civilians. It doesn't work for cops. My people can't help but use excess force sometimes."

"That's outrageous," said one of the more aggressive students. "They have to learn to keep their hands off people when force isn't required, and they have to back off once they have someone under control."

"That's what we tell our people all the time," the sergeant said, his shoulders drooping in apparent frustration. "The problem is, police have to make decisions very fast. We have to guess whether force is needed, and how much. If the DA's office tried my people every time they guessed wrong, I wouldn't have anyone left to send out on patrol."

"That's what I was trying to say," the DA said, seeming to feel she had stepped onto solid ground. "Police in some neighborhoods have to use force every day. They can't be perfect."

"So you just leave them alone?" another student asked.

"No, I don't. When I get the right case, I prosecute. Last year, I convicted a patrolman for manslaughter after he shot an unarmed kid. The guy panicked and forgot all his training. There wasn't any question that I'd prosecute him."

WHEN BERG GOT BACK TO HIS OFFICE AFTER CLASS, IRENE TOLD HIM his wife had called.

He stood by his desk and punched her number into his phone. "Hello, what's up?" Berg asked when Eve answered.

"I talked to my friend in the chemistry department. Evidently there's a situation over there that's an open secret, but she doesn't know if Willard was involved."

"What are we talking about?"

"I'm not sure I want to tell you," Eve said, laughing softly.

"Sounds interesting."

"'Interesting' is too mild for this. There's a graduate student over there who can't get enough sex, though as I understand it, she tries. It evidently goes on in offices and in labs."

"No wonder chemistry has become a popular major," Berg offered, trying to be funny.

"It's not funny, knucklehead. The woman has a real problem." Eve paused and sighed before going on. "Anyway, I asked about professors being involved. My friend says there are stories that the woman has been with some of the professors, including more than one at the same time. The actual same time, my friend says. She doesn't know about Willard. She said she wouldn't put it past him, though."

"Thanks for the information. I'll have to check into it. Did you get the woman's name?"

"I bet you'll check into it. You just watch how you check into it. Her name is Janet Miller."

Berg wondered if the story of Janet Miller was one of the things the chair of the chemistry department had been trying to hide the day before, and he thought he might as well find out. He pushed the now familiar telephone buttons for James Lerner's number and got him on the line.

"Jim, Eric Berg. About our conversation yesterday." Berg stopped, letting Lerner hang on the line.

"Yes," Lerner said, after an uncomfortable silence. "What about it?"

"There are some problems. I'm going to come over and talk to you about them. Is now okay?"

"I suppose so," said Lerner nervously, not knowing what Berg was up to. "Come on over."

When Berg walked into Lerner's office a few minutes later, he found Lerner less confident than before. No longer did he play the expert, as he had when showing Berg how chemists work with fume hoods.

"Is Janet Miller the reason you were uncomfortable talking about whether Frank Willard had behaved himself?" Berg began when they had sat down.

"Well," Lerner said, drawing the word out, "yes. I can tell you that she's a very appealing woman, but I don't know for sure if Frank had even met her."

Berg wondered why Lerner had added his appraisal of Janet Miller. Maybe because of his own involvement with her, he guessed. Perhaps sensing that Berg might draw that conclusion, Lerner went on.

"Don't get the wrong idea. I admit that if I were around her much I'd be tempted, but it would be pretty stupid. I'm afraid the stories are going to get around the university, and that's not going to do the department any good. If I were involved, I'd for sure be forced to step down as chair."

"I can buy that, but why did you lie to me about how well you knew Willard's widow, about how you got to know her, and so on?"

"Who said I lied?

"No one said so, but I've found it out nevertheless.

"How?" Lerner asked, seeming to Berg to be more interested in how he had been caught in a lie that the fact that Berg had caught him.

"Take a look at this," Berg said, tossing Willard's file on his desk.

Berg sat quietly, watching Lerner's expressions and body movements as he turned over the pages in the file. He didn't seem to Berg to be too concerned until he got to the documents that showed his misuse of funds. Then he ran his hand through his hair as he stood up from his desk and began pacing around his office.

Finally Lerner said, "I really can't tell you why I wasn't more forthcoming about my relationship with Willard's wife. It was a long time ago, and I was dating my current wife at the same time. I guess I didn't want it to get out that she wasn't my number one choice."

"Did you know that Willard had it in for you?"

"I knew he didn't consider me a friend, but I had no idea he'd been keeping a file on me."

"He never threatened you with it?" Berg asked, watching Lerner's response carefully. He noticed that before Lerner answered he drew his lips up and wrinkled his brow just a little bit. Small but tell-tale signs of deceit.

"No," Lerner said. He never gave me any indication that he had a file or that he would use it against me."

"Let's cut the crap, Jim. You may think I'm an amateur, but it doesn't take a New York homicide detective to tell that you're lying. Don't dig yourself into a hole. Once you lie to a cop he won't believe you if you tell him it's cold in January." Then, after a bit of silence, Berg said, "I've got to warn you, I'm beginning to suspect you of Willard's murder."

"Okay, he said he was watching me and keeping a file, but I didn't know what was in it. I assumed it was mostly that piddly stuff about Marilyn Harris. And I certainly didn't kill him."

"So what's got you afraid? You're not pacing around here because you need the exercise. Any idiot could see that you're scared."

"It's the stuff about grants. I had no idea Willard had those documents, and I can't figure out how he got them."

Berg had continued to watch Lerner for signs of lying, but he wasn't enough of an expert to pick up on the subtleties. Berg just didn't know what to think about Lerner.

"Well, I'll tell you, Jim. I'd like to believe you. I'm going to try to believe you. But we'll just have to see."

"What about the file?" Lerner asked. "What are you going to do with it? You know it could get me fired as chair?"

"Maybe, but lots of university administrators have played the same game."

"Yes, but suddenly the rules have changed. What the government winked at one day it found shocking the next."

"I'm not a government auditor. What's in the file is of no interest to me—unless it turns out to have something to do with Willard's death. If it doesn't, the file will gather dust in a forgotten corner of my office."

"Thank you for that," Lerner said, looking to Berg like a man who'd gotten a reprieve.

After Berg had finished with Lerner, having failed to clear away his doubts about him, Berg couldn't resist checking further into the story of Janet Miller. That, at least, should prove interesting, Berg thought. The question was, how to proceed?

Berg walked to his car trying to figure out whether he had any option other than simply confronting Janet Miller directly about her possible involvement with Willard. He knew that investigators should postpone interviews until they have the best ammunition. That was why he hadn't yet interviewed Willard's widow.

The only evidence Berg thought he might find of Willard's involvement with the student would be telephone records. Periodically the university rebid its contract for a telephone system, and Berg knew that the business office collected data on telephone usage to help figure out the university's needs. He decided to see if he could get some help from them.

"Hello," Berg said, showing his credentials to the woman behind the counter. "I'm with the university police, and I need some help. If I give you a university extension number, do you have records that will show calls?"

"We don't have them, but we can get the computer to generate them. We can only get outgoing calls, though, not incoming."

"That's okay," Berg said. "If you'll give me a university directory, I'll look up the number. Maybe you could go back, say, three months."

Berg found Willard's office extension and gave it to the clerk. He then wrote down the telephone number of Janet Miller's apartment so he could look for it on the computer list. Barely two minutes later the clerk handed him a computer printout showing all calls from Willard's office in the past three months. Berg quickly fingered down the list, looking for Janet Miller's number. It was there, several times.

He thumbed through the university directory again and found her address, then decided to check her apartment after lunch, on the chance that she would be home. He stopped at the faculty club and sat at the same table as Monday. As he expected, most of Monday's crowd was there. Berg realized that he wanted to tell them the gossip he'd picked up about the chemistry department. He knew they would love it. But he kept his mouth shut.

The Labcoat

Berg hurriedly ate the last of his lunch and then drove the mile or so to Janet Miller's apartment, going faster than he should have because he wasn't paying attention to his driving. The woman was too much on his mind. What would she be like? he wondered. And would he find her at home? More important, would she be alone? From what Eve had said, it didn't sound like Janet Miller spent much time alone.

The apartment was in a complex on the edge of the campus called University Place. Berg had never been there before, but he knew to expect the cheapest construction that would meet building codes and minimal maintenance. As he climbed the stairs to the second floor, he knew he had called it right. He could see all the seams in the drywall because the owners evidently weren't willing to pay for a proper finishing job.

Berg found her apartment and knocked. Until Janet Miller opened the door, Berg hadn't decided how he would play the interview. "Janet?" he began.

"Yes."

"I'm Eric Berg. I'm in the biology department. Frank Willard said I should be sure to meet you, and I thought I would stop by to see if you were home. He was going to introduce us, but, well, he didn't get a chance. May I come in?"

"Okay," she said, opening the door and standing aside. "It was terrible about Frank."

As Berg moved past her, he understood why Lerner called Janet Miller appealing. Actually, "luscious" was the word that came to Berg's mind. She was five foot two, short brown hair, early twenties. Hint of baby fat. Breasts that strained her pale blue cotton blouse. He tried not to stare at them as he stepped past her.

What he looked at mostly was her face. From what he had heard about her, Berg had expected a hard edge, but he didn't find it. Everything about her face was soft, and he couldn't help focusing on her eyes. Big, round, brown. Dreamy. Doe eyes, he thought to himself, though until that moment he hadn't known what doe eyes were.

Janet shut the door and took the couple of steps needed to put her almost up against Berg, closer by a foot and a half than most women would stand. She looked up at him and said teasingly,

"What did Frank tell you about me?"

"He said you were the best lover he ever had."

"He seemed to like it," Janet said, breaking into a little smile and swinging her right shoulder a couple of inches toward him, just brushing up against his sports jacket.

Berg wasn't looking at her eyes now. With Janet almost pressed against him, he couldn't help look beyond her eyes to her breasts. She broadened her smile as she put her left hand to the top button of her blouse and said, "Would you like to see them?"

Berg could feel his heart pick up speed as if he'd been given a shot of adrenaline, and his mouth began to go dry. Did he want to see them? At that moment, there was nothing in the world he wanted as much as to see Janet Miller's breasts. As he tried to figure out what to say, Janet unbuttoned the top three buttons of her blouse, setting Berg's heart running even faster as she gave him a full view of the top of her breasts, outlined by her low-cut, white lace bra. As she moved her hand away from the buttons on her blouse she began to caress the right side of Berg's chest.

He let out the involuntary sigh of a defeated man, just as Janet felt the gun he was carrying on his right hip.

"What's this?" she said in a stronger voice. Before he could answer, she unbuttoned his sports coat and pulled it open on the right side, now substituting a new question, "What are you?"

Berg took a step back and brought his credentials case out of the inside left pocket of his coat. He held it open for her and said, "I'm with the university police."

"Great," Janet said with a mixture of disgust and fear, as she rebuttoned her blouse. "Are you going to arrest me?"

"What for?"

"I don't know. What are you here for?"

"I assure you, I have no intention of arresting you. I'm investigating Frank Willard's death. I didn't tell you who I was because I was trying to keep it from getting out that there is any question about his death." This last was, in fact, just Berg's lame excuse for the play acting he'd done.

"What question is there? I thought he died of a heart attack."

"He may have, but I doubt it. I'd like to talk to you about it, if you'll promise to keep the discussion to yourself."

"Okay, why not," Janet said, seeming to get her confidence back.

"Why don't we sit down?" Berg suggested, leading Janet to a chair while he took a place on the adjoining couch. "How long had you been seeing Frank Willard?"

"For the last few months."

"Do you think his wife knew?"

"No, I don't think so. He was pretty careful. We came over here during the day when he didn't think she would know where he might be."

"Do you know what their relationship was like?"

"Not really. He didn't talk about her much." That Berg could imagine.

"Did you ever get the idea that he thought she was fooling around too?"

"Once he said something. I can't remember what it was exactly, but I got the idea he had caught her seeing someone else."

As Berg listened, he looked around the room. Standard graduate student decor. The furniture was cheap and looked secondhand, but the stereo equipment was new, including a VCR. Seeing that caused Berg to wonder. "Did Frank ever bring X-rated videos to watch?"

"Yes, sometimes. There were a couple he brought."

That seemed to answer the question Berg had about why Willard kept the videos in his office rather than at home. He evidently didn't watch them at home.

"I've got one more question," Berg said, deciding he'd make a guess that might or might not be right. "I want to know who was here with Frank."

"Gee, I don't want to tell you that. I don't want to get anyone in trouble."

"I understand," Berg said, glad that he'd asked the question. "But I think Frank was murdered, and I don't have much in the way of leads. I need your help."

"The guy we used to, uh, be here with," Janet said, struggling for a polite way to put it, "didn't kill him. I can tell you that."

"I'm sure you're right about that, but he may be the best source of information I have about Frank and his wife.

Considering the circumstances, I thought that maybe Frank would have talked to him about his wife having an affair or about whether he thought his wife knew about you. Look, I'll tell you what, you give me his name and I promise it won't go any further. You won't be causing him any trouble, and maybe he can help."

"All right," Janet said uncertainly, after a pause. "Charles Gleason. He's an associate professor in the chemistry department."

"Thanks," Berg told her, getting up to leave. "Can I give you a couple bits of advice?"

"Sure."

"I used to be the pastor of a church. I didn't come here to preach to you, but I don't want to leave without telling you that your behavior is self-destructive. It will catch up with you sooner or later."

"I know," Janet said sadly, her eyes pointed at the floor. "I'm working on it."

"Good. You're also too trusting. Don't let guys you don't know in the door. You don't know what weirdos may show up."

"I know that too," Janet said, looking up at Berg and smiling.

As he drove back to the university, Berg wondered what would have happened if he had left his gun at his office. He knew for sure what would have happened twenty years before. Was he any wiser now or just older? Berg didn't know. Now he found himself driving more slowly than usual, because Janet Miller had drained him emotionally.

He decided to stop at the chemistry department and see if he could find Charles Gleason. Maybe Gleason could tell him something useful about Willard's wife. Berg had now been to the chemistry department enough to know his way around, including that there was a board on the wall near the first floor elevator that listed names of professors and office numbers. He stopped there and then rode the elevator to the fifth floor, jammed in with undergraduates, a couple almost as appealing as Janet Miller. Gleason was in his office grading exams.

"Professor Gleason," Berg began, flipping open his credentials case for Gleason to see, "I'm Assistant Chief Berg of the university police. I need to speak with you."

Gleason looked uneasy, but motioned him to a chair. Berg nodded and closed the door behind him.

"My hope is that you may be able to tell me something about Frank Willard's situation with his wife. Do you think she knew about Frank's relationship with Janet Miller?"

"How do you know about that?" Gleason said. His whole body seemed to jump.

"Well, I'm an investigator. You don't think it would be too difficult to find out about that, do you?"

"I don't suppose so," Gleason said. "I don't have any reason to believe his wife knew about Janet Miller."

"What about yours?" Berg asked, noticing Gleason's wedding ring.

"No, she doesn't know."

"Did you and Frank Willard talk about the problem of your wives finding out?"

"Yeah, we were both worried about it."

"What about Doris Willard? Did Frank think she was seeing anyone on the side?"

"Not that I know of. I don't think she and Frank were very close, though. Perhaps the differences in their ages had something to do with it, but I don't know."

"All right, thanks for your help. By the way, don't tell anyone I've asked you these questions, okay?"

"That's fine with me. You're not going to tell anyone about Janet and me, are you?"

"No, but with her appetite for sex and everybody else's for gossip, I wouldn't give a dollar to a hundred on the university president not finding out, no less anyone else around here."

From the sick look on Gleason's face, Berg could see that Gleason agreed.

"One more thing," Berg added coldly, with his eyes locked on Gleason's. "When the time comes for the piper to be paid, make sure Janet Miller's not the one who does the paying."

Chapter Eight

BY THE NEXT DAY IT WAS PERFECTLY CLEAR TO BERG THAT HE HAD DONE ALL THE preparation he could before interviewing Doris Willard. Somehow he didn't want to deliver Willard's belongings in the paper bag the funeral director had given him, so he climbed the stairs to the attic of his house and found a plain white box that a blouse for Eve had come in last Christmas. On his way to the university, Berg dropped by Willard's house, hoping to find Doris Willard at home.

The house was in the "University Ghetto," an area next to the university where most of the residences were owned by professors and administrators. The Willard house was typical, but one of the nicer. It was a story and a half, with white painted brick and dark brown shutters, its style a cross between Williamsburg and New England colonial. The grass needed to be cut—he guessed that cutting the grass had been Frank Willard's job.

Berg walked to the front door, white box in hand. "Hello, Mrs. Willard," Berg began when Doris Willard opened the door, "I'm Eric Berg. I teach at the Divinity School, and I also do some work with the university police. I have some of your husband's things here. May I come in?"

"Yes, all right," Doris said, opening the door wider and standing aside. Upon stepping in, he found himself in the living room, and was immediately impressed with someone's taste. Doris Willard's, he guessed, because the room was definitely feminine, done in light greens and pinks, with ruffled throw pillows. "Why don't you sit down here on the sofa," she continued, motioning to him with her hand. "I know I'm going to have to go over to Frank's office and clean it out, but I haven't felt up to it."

"I'm sure there's no hurry about that. I have Frank's keys here, though, so you can get into the building and his office anytime you want." Berg handed the box over. "You have his wallet here too, and everything else he had with him when he died."

"Thank you," she said, forcing a smile as she took the box.

So far, she seemed to fit Berg's idea of the typical grieving widow, except that he found her to be an unusually attractive one. She had a trim, mildly athletic build that fit what Lerner had said about her and tennis. She must be careful to shield herself from the sun, he thought, because her forty-something face was almost unlined, and she was pretty in a younger way than most attractive women her age.

Berg didn't feel comfortable with the questions he had to ask, but he started out as gently as he was capable of. "You probably don't know this," he began, "but we haven't been able to close the police report on your husband's death. In cases like this the medical examiner's office usually does an autopsy, or at least examines the body, but that wasn't done. So I'm afraid I need to ask you some questions."

"All right," Doris said, seemingly without emotion, but looking at Berg with eyes that to him appeared maybe to have some sparkle in them.

"The big question the medical examiner's office wants to have answered, I guess, is why there was a hurry to have the body cremated?"

"I don't know," Doris said, shifting her body in her chair and crossing her legs before leaning forward towards Berg. "I saw him lying on a metal cart in the emergency room and I wanted him out of there. I didn't want to think of him lying on a slab at the funeral home."

Berg couldn't tell what he was hearing. He wasn't picking up any emotion, and he didn't know what to make of it. He began to wish that he had brought someone else along to help him evaluate what he was hearing and seeing, preferably a woman. For one thing, he knew his male urges were getting in the way. Like most men, he found vulnerability in women to be provocative, and Doris was showing vulnerability. All Berg could do now was salvage the interview as best he could.

"I know the university personnel office will help you with some papers you have to file and so on," he began again, struggling for a delicate way to get an answer to his next question. "Do you know how much insurance Frank had?"

He could tell he had hit a nerve. Doris drew back slightly and frowned, then tugged at her skirt, pulling it down further over her knees. She looked at Berg sharply, but all she said was, "Whatever he had through the university. I don't know."

"Do you know of anyone who may have had a motive to kill him?"

"No. Absolutely not."

"One last question," Berg said, getting up to leave.

Doris got up too, and as she did she ran her hands over her dress, starting just under her breasts and ending at mid-thighs. Berg was taken aback, but he told himself that he wasn't in the best position to tell the difference between a sexually suggestive gesture and a woman merely straightening her dress.

"Who told you Frank had been taken to the emergency room?" Berg asked.

"A woman from his department called and said he had fallen on the stairs and that he was being taken to University Hospital."

"Can you give me her name?"

"No, I don't know who she was. She probably said her name, but I didn't pay any attention. One of the secretaries, I guess."

He told Doris Willard he was sorry about her husband's death, then excused himself and went to his car. He didn't know what to make of her. He certainly hadn't eliminated her as a suspect, but he hadn't found out anything that pointed to her either. All he had learned was that he found her very attractive.

Berg's mention to Doris Willard of the university personnel office gave him the idea that they could tell him something about Willard's life insurance, so he pointed his car there. The personnel office was on a side street that literally had repairs on top of repairs. He grimaced as the wide tires of his Corvette hit the bumps, jarring his spine and setting his nerves on edge.

Once in the building, he was handed off twice from one clerk to another until he found himself in the office of the benefits administrator. She was able to tell him from Willard's computer file that the professor had carried the maximum insurance offered through the university, an amount equal to twice his salary. Fifty thousand of that was provided by the university, and the rest, totaling well over a hundred thousand more, had been paid by Willard through payroll deductions. Doris Willard was the beneficiary.

People have been killed for less, Berg thought, but, on the other hand, if Doris Willard had never worked, Berg knew that she could get alimony in a divorce, at least for some years. That struck him as a better deal than murder for life insurance equal to two year's salary.

He wondered, though, whether there was life insurance he didn't know about. He carried the maximum university insurance, but didn't consider it enough. The best deal he had been able to find on additional insurance was from the Teachers Insurance and Annuity Association, which managed the university's pension funds. Berg figured that Willard, if he had wanted additional insurance, likely would have gone to TIAA.

"Do you ever talk to TIAA about insurance they write on professors?" Berg said to the benefits administrator.

"No, I've never had occasion to."

"How'd you like to play detective?" Berg asked, smiling and trying to make his offer sound intriguing. "I'd like you to call them and see if you can find out if they carried insurance on Frank Willard."

"I'm not sure they'll tell me."

"I'm not sure either, but you'll have a better chance with them than I would. You could tell them that his widow doesn't know about any insurance, which is what she told me, and that you want to help her by finding out if there is any."

The chance to play detective was too good to turn down, so the benefits administrator got TIAA on the telephone. After giving a clerk in the life insurance department the university's account number and Willard's social security number, the administrator waited a few seconds and then put her hand over the phone and turned to Berg. "He had a $150 thousand policy, naming his wife as beneficiary." Then, turning back to the telephone, she listened for maybe fifteen seconds and said, "Okay, thanks very much. I'll pass the information on to his widow."

After hanging up, the administrator gave Berg more good news for Doris Willard. The policy had been written more than a decade earlier, and it had an inflation rider. Its value now was over $300 thousand.

If you didn't like your husband much to start with, Berg thought, almost a half million dollars was certainly enough to kill for. The question is, did Doris Willard know about the insurance. "Let's play detective a little more," Berg said. "You should give Willard's widow the good news anyway. Why don't you call her and tell her about the university's policy and the TIAA policy. She won't know whether you usually have that information or not. I can listen in on another extension and see if I can tell whether she knew about the insurance."

The benefits administrator was less sure about this phone call, but agreed.

"Mrs. Willard, this is the benefits administrator at the university," she began when Doris Willard answered the phone. "I'm sorry about the loss of your husband."

Berg waited as Doris Willard gave a polite response.

"Is this an okay time to talk to you about his insurance?"

"I guess so."

"Well, he had a policy through the university that will pay twice his current salary. I will send you some papers to sign about that."

"Okay, thank you."

So far, Berg noticed, he was still hearing the same show-no-emotion response.

"Also, your husband had a policy with TIAA. It will pay something over $300 thousand."

"Really?" Doris Willard said, her voice brightening. "I didn't know about that."

After the benefits administrator told Doris Willard how to contact TIAA and had hung up, Berg asked her if she thought Mrs. Willard had actually been surprised.

"She sounded like it to me, but you're the detective," she told him.

That didn't make Berg feel any better, because he had no idea how to tell if Mrs. Willard's surprise had been genuine. It seemed to him that it wouldn't take an Academy Award performance to sound like she had on the telephone, so he didn't feel like he'd learned much. He thought Doris Willard was smart, and maybe that was all she had been. He had hoped that she wouldn't show any surprise. Then he might have had something.

Berg had already driven halfway down the block when an idea came to him. Obviously someone had been paying insurance premiums to TIAA for over ten years. He wondered who wrote the checks in Willard's family. If he could find out that it was Doris

Willard, then he'd have something after all. He turned around and went back to the benefit administrator's office.

"One more thing," Berg began as he walked into the office, trying to sound plaintive. "Would you check the records and tell me if Willard had his monthly check sent directly to his bank?"

He had good reason for hope here. A couple of years ago, the university and local banks had run a campaign for direct deposits because it saved them all a lot of fooling around with checks.

"Yes, he did," the benefits administrator said, looking up after working a few computer keys. "First National."

"Great. Give me what the computer shows as Willard's account number at the bank, will you? I'll probably need it."

The number in hand, Berg suddenly felt better. He knew that banks microfilm all checks written on their accounts. If he could talk the bank into cooperating, he could get a look at the microfilms of Willard's canceled checks.

Getting the bank's cooperation took some doing. Berg first drove to the main branch, thinking the microfilm was probably kept there. He soon found out something he should have been smart enough to think of himself—banks don't use expensive downtown space for storage. The main branch sent him to a warehouse on the edge of the city. When he drove up, he saw no sign saying the building was owned by the bank. He assumed the bank didn't want to attract burglars.

Once inside, he showed his credentials and was led into the small, plain office of the head custodian of the records. Berg never did know what his title was, but he could see from the plate on the desk that the man's name was Henry Tanner. Tanner looked to be in his late fifties—paunchy and pasty-faced. It was apparent right away that Tanner wasn't going to be helpful if he could manage to be otherwise.

"I don't see how I can let you look at a customer's microfilms without his permission," Tanner said, with a sharpness to his voice.

"I told you, the account holder is dead," Berg replied, omitting the fact that the account probably was a joint account, with one holder still alive. "This is a murder investigation, and you're in charge of the records."

"Yes, and I say you can't look at them."

"Give me that phone," Berg said, grabbing it from in front of Tanner. "Who do you work for?"

Tanner gave the name and Berg punched "O." As he hoped, that got him the bank's main switchboard, and he asked to be connected to Tanner's superior.

"Hello, Mr. Blaine," Berg began, trying to control his anger, but being only partly successful. "This is Assistant Chief Berg of the university police. I'm down at the warehouse with Henry Tanner. I need access to microfilm records of a deceased person's account in connection with a murder case, and he's jerking me around."

"Well, we consider those records confidential."

"Yes, so do I, to a point. But not in a murder investigation. What do you think the guy's going to do, come back and complain?"

"Perhaps you should get the probate judge's permission."

"I'll tell you what I'm going to do before I talk to a judge," Berg hissed into the phone, his temper blown. "I'm going to arrest the moron you've got running this warehouse for obstruction of justice."

Berg knew that most people didn't have any idea what obstruction of justice was, which made it a good thing to threaten them with. "Besides," Berg added, cooling down a little after making his threat, "the university's one of the bank's biggest customers. Before I do anything else, I'm going to call the bank officer who's in charge of the university's account and see if she doesn't make better sense than Tanner here."

One of Berg's ploys worked, because the next thing he heard was, "You say the account holder is dead?"

"Yes, that's right," Berg said politely. "I have his account number right here."

"Read it to me."

Berg complied and waited as he heard over the telephone the clicking of computer keys.

"It's a joint account with Mr. Willard's wife," the bank officer began.

"Yes, I'm sure it is," Berg said, breaking in before the bank officer could commit himself to turning Berg down. "The problem is, and you need to keep this to yourself," Berg said conspiratorially, "she's the prime suspect." Berg guessed that, if nothing else worked, the chance to be part of a little police work would hook Blaine the way it had the benefits administrator, and he was right.

"Ah yes, I understand. I'm sure we can help under those circumstances. Let me check something for you, though." In a few seconds Blaine continued, "I've got a better idea than microfilm. We store the checks for that account. We have them in the warehouse too. If you'll put Mr. Tanner on the phone, I'll authorize him to let you look at them."

While Tanner got his instructions, Berg recalled a letter he'd received from his bank. It had offered him the same deal: the bank would store his checks rather than send them to him each month. He hadn't been interested because he used the checks as income tax records.

After Tanner put down his phone, he was more cooperative. He brought Berg the last two years of checks from Willard's account and let him use his office to look at them.

"Bingo!" Berg exclaimed to himself, when he found that Doris Willard was the one who paid bills, including writing a check twice a year to TIAA. She had to have known about the insurance and had, for some reason, chosen to try to con him and the benefits administrator. He couldn't think of a better reason than covering up a murder.

On his drive back to his office, Berg thought for the first time about how badly he had fouled-up by bullying his way past Tanner. The guy actually had been doing him a favor without knowing it. By looking through the checks without a search warrant or Doris Willard's permission, Berg probably had insured that what he'd found couldn't be used against her. Pretty stupid mistake for an assistant chief to make, Berg thought to himself.

Chapter Nine

BERG SPENT MOST OF THE FOLLOWING MORNING WONDERING WHAT TO DO ABOUT the Willard investigation. He stopped his ruminations long enough to teach his class on the theology of the early church, or at least he tried to. He found, though, that when his students talked, he couldn't keep his mind on what they were saying. Thoughts about the Willard case kept interrupting.

Willard's death clearly looked to be murder. Even so, Berg had to wonder if there was something he was missing. Perhaps

Willard had died from a heart attack after all. Thinking back to his few minutes with Janet Miller, Berg wondered whether an overweight, middle-aged guy with a bad heart could hope to stand the excitement he knew the woman had provided. Maybe Willard blew an artery from his heart just thinking about what Janet Miller did for him and his friend Gleason.

Assuming Willard had been murdered, though, where was he in the way of suspects? There was the problem. He had too many suspects. Doris Willard, of course, was at the top of the list because of motive, her pushing for a quick cremation, and her lying about Willard's life insurance.

Then, Marilyn Harris. She had reported finding the body, which cracked open the drapes of suspicion only the tiniest bit and wouldn't have made any difference by itself. But the drapes got pulled back further because of the disappearance of Willard's books, which hadn't been put where she said they would, and because of her weird relationship with Willard. From what Lerner had told him, about the destroyed manuscript chapters and his suspicions when he had talked to her about them, it seemed that for some unknown reason she had hated Willard mightily.

Then, as much as Berg didn't want to come to it, there was Lerner himself. Willard's evidence of the grant funds misuse was an excellent motive for getting him out of the way. Lerner was right to think he could get fired as chair over that, and, though he said he didn't know Willard had the evidence against him, Berg had caught him lying at least twice.

Each of the three would have to be investigated further, Berg knew, starting with Doris Willard. The trouble with his investigation of her, though, was that he hadn't found anything that either pointed straight at her or cleared her, and he didn't know what else to do.

Berg wished he'd been able to find out if she knew Willard was fooling around on her, and he also wished he'd been able to learn about her possible love interest. All he had there was Janet Miller's belief that Willard had caught his wife seeing someone else.

There was another question he knew he hadn't gotten to the bottom of—how Doris Willard knew her husband had been taken to University Hospital. Her story of being called by an unknown woman in the chemistry department might or might not be true. Berg could check, but it would stir up rumors in the department, and he wanted to avoid that for the moment. Anyway, he was inclined to believe that part of Doris Willard's story. If she had killed her husband, or had someone do it, he figured she would have sat tight until she got the inevitable phone call. To do anything else would have been stupid, and he didn't think Doris Willard was stupid.

One day a week, Berg and his wife had lunch together, and he tried to put this thoughts about the Willard case aside as he drove to meet Eve. He always looked forward to these lunches. He now wondered if that was because, when they first started having them, he and Eve would have lunch and then go home and spend an hour in bed. That was during the years when their boys, Rob and Hugh, were in grade school, and they'd found that the middle of a school day was the best time for lovemaking. Now Hugh was in high school, and rarely home day or evening, and Rob was away at college. Sneaking away wasn't necessary anymore.

Today they had agreed to meet at the Rangoon. Eve was there when Berg arrived, five minutes late.

"Sorry," he said as he sat down across from her at the table for two the waiter had led him to. "I let the time slip away from me."

"That's okay," Eve said, smiling. "I was going to give you at least another five minutes before I looked around for someone more interesting."

Berg picked up the menu the waiter had left in front of him. His chair faced a large, plate glass window, and he alternated between looking at the menu and peering over the top of it at Eve and at the scene in the window behind her. A thunderstorm had been moving in as he drove to the restaurant, and now it framed Eve's body with a boiling, heaving black cloud and added highlights to her hair with flashes of lightning.

"Why are you sitting there with your mouth hanging open?" Eve asked.

"I was just thinking about how beautiful you are."

"Likely story. I know you. You were probably thinking about the chicken vandaloo."

"No, no," Berg said, defending himself. "I really was thinking about how beautiful you are." But, even though he did think that often, it was not what he had been thinking as he looked out the window. What he had been thinking about was how Eve would swoop down on him like a female Thor if she caught him fooling around with Janet Miller or Doris Willard, which he knew he'd be tempted to try if his judgment weakened any.

After ordering, Berg began talking about the Willard case. He felt sure Willard had been murdered, he told Eve, but he still had no idea how someone could have poisoned him on the stairway. "You're the scientist," he said. "How could someone have killed him in the stairwell with cyanide?"

"That's an engineering problem. There's no science to it."

"Well, still. Help me figure it out. Somehow, someone evidently found a way to hit him with cyanide. Vapor or spray, the crime lab says."

"And without killing himself. That's important," she added, starting to show interest in working out the puzzle.

"I've tried to think about how cyanide has been used to kill people. Mainly, there's the gas chamber."

"I guess you could turn the stairwell into a gas chamber," Eve said pensively. Then she quickly added, "But that didn't happen. Too dangerous."

"Also, the stuff was only on the top part of the labcoat," Berg said. "You read about spies killing themselves with cyanide capsules. But a capsule is what I had in mind when I told the lab to check for residue from Willard's mouth. I thought someone might have shoved one in and chucked him in the jaw."

"I don't know," Eve said with resignation, as if she were giving up on the problem. "It sounds like spy stuff to me. Maybe Willard had worked for the KGB and his past caught up with him."

"Nah," Berg said, taking his wife seriously for a second before he saw that she was joking.

"It does sound like spy stuff, though," Eve began again. "You said it all sounded new to the crime lab people. Maybe that's because it is spy stuff. Why don't you go to the library and do some research in spy books?"

"It's a good idea, I guess. But I'm too lazy. I could get one of my research assistants to do it. Couldn't hurt."

"Good. What's for dessert?"

"I've been thinking," Berg said. "What about going home for awhile? Remember how we used to have 'French dessert?'"

"I remember," Eve said as she caught the waiter's eye to ask for their check. "How much time do you have before class?"

BERG ARRIVED BACK AT HIS OFFICE JUST BEFORE HIS THREE O'CLOCK class, not much interested in thinking just then about Janet Miller or Doris Willard. Without knowing it, Eve had seen to that. Berg asked his secretary to find Jane Samuels and have her meet him in his office at four o'clock. When he walked in after class, she was already there.

"I've got a job for you," he began. "How'd you like to read some spy stuff?"

"Probably be more interesting than what I've been doing. What do you need done?"

"You remember the professor who died over in the chemistry building last week, supposedly from a heart attack?" Berg said, knowing Jane would have more enthusiasm for the research if she knew why she was doing it. "I was talking about it on the phone when you were here the other day."

"I remember."

"He probably was murdered as he walked up the stairway. You need to help me figure out how."

"What do I look for?" Jane asked, the expression on her face showing her interest.

"Some way to kill a person with cyanide, vapor or spray, that would expose only the top of the body to the stuff. It has to be portable, and something that would work in a public, or at least semi-public, place. The state police crime lab has evidently never seen anything that would do it, so maybe the killer got the idea from something to do with spies."

"Or maybe he thought it up himself," Jane said.

"That too. In which case we're probably out of luck in learning how it was done."

"Do you have an idea on how I should start?"

"Not much of one. You've become a better researcher than I am. I'd go to the main university library first, but you may have to go to the public library downtown. They'll probably have more popular stuff. I'd try books and magazines. You might try the *New York Times* index too. They have that in the reference room at the main library, and they've got the newspaper going all the way back on microfilm."

"Yes, I know. They've got all sorts of stuff on the computer too. When do you want this?"

"ASAP. Maybe we've got a KGB-type assassin running around loose on campus," Berg said, trying to sound funny.

"I'll spend the weekend on it."

Chapter Ten

EARLIER IN THE WEEK, EVE HAD INSISTED THEY NEEDED TO GET AWAY. SHE WANTED to see Rob, who was at Northwestern, and spend a weekend in Chicago. Plus, she said, Berg needed a rest. He had agreed, but when Friday night came, he argued that he needed to work on the Willard case and catch up at the Divinity School. Eve said they should stick to the original plan and, as usual, she won.

Though they could have gone to Chicago by airline, Berg thought it would be more fun to fly himself. When a young Army officer, he had learned to fly, and he still sometimes flew a rented plane. The plan was to fly to Chicago Saturday morning and back Sunday evening.

Like all pilots, Berg had learned to pay attention to the weather. On Saturday, the FAA briefer told him the forecast for the morning was for a two-thousand-foot layer of clouds beginning at three thousand feet, and clear above. Then some thicker clouds as they got nearer Chicago, with widely scattered thunderstorms. Satisfied with the weather, he filed an instrument flight plan.

Berg drove to the airport first, at eight Saturday morning, so he could get the plane ready before Eve arrived. He liked to take his time at that, and he felt rushed if anyone was waiting.

When Berg got to the airport, he looked carefully at the sky, studying all quadrants. It was overcast, as expected, but with lots of light coming through. That told him the forecast of a two-thousand-foot cloud deck had come true. Had the sky been dark gray, he would have known the clouds were much thicker.

Berg took the keys off the peg where they hung and walked to the airplane, which the line crew had pulled out of the big hangar it shared with fifteen others. The plane was a Rockwell Commander with the registration number N4824W. He checked it carefully, opening access doors and crouching down to look under the wheel wells. Whoever had flown it last had noted no problems, and he found none either.

Berg told the man who drove the fuel truck that he wanted full fuel, enough for over five hours. He believed you couldn't carry too much fuel, and he always flew with full tanks unless it would put the airplane over its allowable weight. There would be no problem with weight on the flight to Chicago, since only two of the airplane's four seats would be filled.

After finishing the ground check, he loaded the suitcases into the baggage compartment, which was accessed through a door on the side of the airplane aft of the left wing. Then he poked around the large hangar, looking at one airplane and then another, not because he was much interested, but because he was too nervous to sit in the pilot's lounge like most pilots did.

The Labcoat

Berg was always nervous before he got going on a flight. He was a careful pilot and good at flying. But there were so many things a pilot could neither foresee nor control. That's why some people liked flying—fighting the challenges—but not Berg. The uncertainties, especially with weather, always bothered him until he started the engine. Then, for some reason, his nervousness went away.

He had figured out that he didn't so much like flying as he liked being a pilot. This came to him one day when a friend asked why he liked to fly airplanes. Berg stumbled around the question, trying to answer it for his friend and, as it turned out, for himself. He ended up telling a story. A visiting general was inspecting airborne troops. As he went down the lines of soldiers standing at attention, he stopped to ask a question.

"Do you like jumping out of airplanes, soldier?"

"No, not me, General. I'm scared to jump out of airplanes."

"Well why in hell did you volunteer for an airborne unit?"

"Because I like to be with men who like to jump out of airplanes."

The story didn't exactly capture Berg's feelings about being a pilot, but it was the best he could do.

EVE ARRIVED AT NINE, AND THEY SET OUT. AS SOON AS THE PLANE lifted off, Berg moved the switches that selected gear and flaps up, and heard through his headset the request from the tower to climb to three thousand feet and contact departure control.

"Departure, four-eight-two-four-whiskey is with you, out of one-point-two for three," Berg said through the microphone attached to his headset.

"Two-four-whiskey, radar contact. Turn right, heading three-three-zero. Climb and maintain six thousand."

"Roger, right to three-three-zero. We're out of one-point-five for six. Two-four-whiskey."

At just about three thousand feet, as advertised by the FAA, the airplane punched into the base of the cloud cover and began to be buffeted by the light turbulence found in clouds that are basically flat stratus, but with a hint of cumulus. Berg went on instruments, keeping the airplane right side up, climbing, and on course by looking at the gauges in the panel in front of him and by making small, precise movements of the control wheel. In less than five minutes, the airplane climbed out of the clouds into bright sunshine. The cloud cover below was a brilliant white from horizon to horizon.

In a half hour, he could see the beginnings of a higher cloud layer ahead. After another hour, the clouds above merged with those below, putting him back on instruments. That would be no problem, as long as there weren't any thunderstorms ahead. No plane could be sure of surviving an encounter with a thunderstorm, and certainly not an airplane the size Berg was flying.

Later, after a long time on instruments, he decided to find out what the controller saw on his radar.

"Indianapolis Center, two-four-whiskey. Are you painting any weather ahead?"

"Negative, two-four-whiskey."

A half hour further on, after being handed off to Chicago Center, the clouds got darker, and the airplane ran into rain. Berg decided to check again.

"Chicago Center, two-four-whiskey. Do you show any cells on our route?"

"Two-four-whiskey, you've got areas of what looks like light to moderate rain for the next few miles. I had a King Air through there ten minutes ago at twelve thousand. He reported only light turbulence."

"Two-four-whiskey, roger. Thanks."

But ten minutes can be half the life of a building thunderstorm cell, as Berg was soon to find out. The clouds turned black around them as the airplane hit rain heavy enough to make Berg fear that the engine would drown. At the same time, they entered a two-thousand-foot-per-minute downdraft. He and Eve were thrown against their seat belts as the airplane rocked violently from side to side in severe turbulence. It seemed to be falling like the air holding it up had given way.

"We're in a cell!" was all he could get out of his mouth, as he wrestled with the control wheel, trying to keep the airplane right side up and headed halfway in the right direction.

As suddenly as they had been forced down, though, losing a thousand feet in half a minute, they hit a rising column of air that threw the plane up like a tin can with a firecracker under it and tried to flip them over and shake them to death at the same time. It was the central core of the storm.

"Turn around! Turn around!" Eve yelled over her headset, with a terror in her voice any sane person would feel.

"I can't," Berg managed to say, his voice shaking as he still fought to keep the airplane in control. Then he added hopefully, "We should be halfway through." Soon the cycle started all over again, as the airplane hit another powerful downdraft. For some reason, Berg turned his head to the right. Beyond the side window were boiling black clouds, lit at the moment by a lightning flash, and he saw Eve outlined by the storm, just as he had in the restaurant window the day before.

In less than another minute, the thunderstorm spit them out into a clear blue sky, the only remaining clouds a stratus deck below.

"I don't care if I ever do that again," Eve said, looking over at Berg and forcing herself to sound lighthearted.

Berg couldn't sound lighthearted because his voice still shook. "You won't have to with me," he told her. "I should have known better than to try it without radar."

Soon Chicago Center handed the airplane off to Chicago Approach, and Berg asked if they could get radar vectors to Meigs Field, a small airport on the shores of Lake Michigan in downtown Chicago, rather than to Midway, where his flight plan said they were going.

"Roger two-four-whiskey. Expect a visual approach to runway three-six. Turn ten degrees right. Descend and maintain three thousand."

"Ten degrees right. We're out of six for three. Two-four-whiskey."

They again entered the clouds while descending, but quickly broke out through the bottom of the overcast and within ten minutes were in sight of the lake. The sky was clear above the water, which was lit by brilliant sunshine that turned it a deep blue.

Rob met them at Meigs, where Berg had told him they would land if the weather was good, and they spent the afternoon together having lunch and looking at the Art Institute of Chicago's collection of Impressionist paintings. Berg was proud of Rob, who was doing well as an English major and was also, from what Berg could piece together, having a good time. They had been close over the years, and Berg missed having him at home.

After Rob took the train to Evanston for a date, Berg and his wife walked to the Berghoff for dinner. Large, multi-leveled, and multi-roomed, the Berghoff was a place where it seemed every visitor to Chicago ended up, a place where tourists waited in line with locals.

Berg sat studying the dessert menu after finishing his beef roulade. He couldn't decide between rice pudding and custard and had just decided to order both when a woman he hadn't noticed before, sitting in the next dining room, stood up and walked away from her table, leaving her male companion behind. Something about the way she straightened her dress caught Berg's eye as she got up. From a distance she looked like Doris Willard, but Berg doubted he'd see her in Chicago.

Berg had a good view of the man who had been left at the table, still eating, but he didn't recognize him. The man was early middle-aged, with a slight build and brown hair, not quite touching his ears, parted near the middle. He wore a brown tweed sportcoat over a blue shirt, opened at the collar. Berg noticed that he kept his fork in his left hand as he ate, marking him either as a European or an American who affected Old World manners.

Berg ordered his two desserts, and Eve one. As they waited for the desserts, he also waited for the return of the woman in the next room. He saw her when she was still twenty feet from her table and got a good enough look before she sat down to be convinced he was looking at Doris Willard.

"I can't believe it," he said.

"What can't you believe?"

The Labcoat

"I'm sure Doris Willard is eating dinner in the next room."

"You've got Doris Willard on your brain," Eve said, waving her hand as if to brush the idea away. "What do you suppose the chance is that she'd come to Chicago the weekend after her husband's funeral, and that you'd happen to run into her at a restaurant?"

"I don't know. Maybe she's come to visit family. There wouldn't be anything strange about that. This is the Berghoff too, you know. Everybody comes to the Berghoff."

"Yes, sure," Eve said with a playful scoff. "Just like in "Casablanca," I suppose, where 'Everybody comes to Rick's.' Next you'll be seeing Major Strasser walk in, dressed in a greatcoat."

"Scoff if you want, but I'm telling you, it's her." Berg didn't add that he was sure because he had paid a lot of attention to how Doris Willard looked when they had met earlier in the week.

"Where is she sitting?" Eve asked, starting to turn around to look into the next room.

"You can't see her face from where you are."

Their desserts came, and they let the subject of Doris Willard go as they began to eat. Then, between bites of rice pudding, Berg noticed that the woman he thought was Doris Willard was holding hands with her companion across their table. It could have been platonic or familial, he thought, but it looked romantic to him.

"Turn around and see if you can get a look at the table along the wall, just before the coat rack," Berg said to Eve. "Is that a couple in love, or what?"

Eve moved her chair sideways so she could look without being obvious. "I'll be," she said, her voice showing surprise as she turned back to face Berg. "That's Francois Beloit. He's in the chemistry department."

"So now do you believe me?" Berg said, trying to sound hurt that Eve had doubted him.

"I'll take your word that it's Doris Willard."

"Am I seeing romance or something else?"

"It sure looked like romance to me." With that Eve turned around again for a quick look. "Romance, definitely," she said.

Berg didn't know what to do, but he wanted to have options. As soon as he could, he caught the eye of the waiter who was standing across the room and made writing motions in the air, indicating that he wanted the check. As he walked to their table, the waiter pulled checks out of his shirt pocket. Berg took his out of the waiter's hand and then reached into his pants pocket for his bills, peeled off enough to cover the bill and tip, and put them on the table. On trips he usually used a credit card, but he had decided he wanted to be ready to follow Doris and her companion when they left the restaurant.

He didn't have long to wait. Soon he saw a waiter bring a check to the table in the next room and then walk away with a credit card.

"It looks like it's no dessert for them—unless it's to be 'French dessert,'" Berg said, leering at Eve.

With the check paid three minutes later, the couple in the next room got up and headed toward the outside door. Berg motioned for Eve to follow, and she walked after him as he moved hurriedly through the dining room. He wanted to stay far enough behind not to be noticed, but close enough to get out the door in time to see which way Doris and her friend had gone.

As he reached the front door, Berg looked through a window and saw the couple step into a taxi. He hurried Eve out the door and was relieved to see a line of waiting taxis. They got into the back seat of the next taxi in line, and Berg took his chance to say the classic line, "Follow that cab!" The problem was, he hammed it up, and the driver thought he was kidding.

"Sorry," Berg said. "I need to know where those people are headed. We'll go wherever they go."

The driver took his role seriously. Berg figured he probably had spent years waiting to hear the words he had spoken. It was a short ride. The taxi they were following made only a couple of turns on its way to the Hyatt Regency, a few blocks north and almost on the lake.

Berg handed the driver some one-dollar bills, and then he and Eve waited in the taxi until they could follow the couple but stay twenty yards behind. As they waited, they watched Francois put his arm around Doris as the two of them walked toward the entrance to the hotel.

"Whatever else they're being," Berg said to no one in particular, "they aren't being careful." Then he turned to Eve. "Would

Francois recognize you?" he said, hoping that she could follow them to their room, if that's where they were going.

"I'm afraid so. We've been on a committee together."

Berg and Eve followed behind, entering the hotel in time to see the couple head for the elevators. They stepped into one that ran to the hotel's lower guest room floors, and Berg decided that was as far as he and Eve could follow.

Chapter Eleven

IT WAS A POSSIBILITY, BERG KNEW, THAT DORIS AND HER FRIEND WERE IN THE HYATT to visit someone, but it didn't look that way to him. To make sure, he walked to the reception desk, Eve with him.

"I'm supposed to meet some friends here," he told the clerk. "Can you check to see if either one of them has arrived yet?"

"Sure, what are their names?"

"Francois Beloit, that's B-e-l-o-i-t," Berg replied, "and Doris Willard."

After a few seconds of typing into a keyboard, the clerk said, "Mr. Beloit checked in this afternoon, and, let's see. No, I don't show anything for a Doris Willard."

"Okay, thanks very much," Berg said, having learned what he had expected to learn. Then he thought of something else, "Say, is Mr. Beloit registered by himself, or is his wife with him?"

"He registered as a single," the clerk told him, looking up from his computer.

"So," Berg said to Eve after they had moved a few steps toward the center of the lobby, "defrauding an innkeeper. He should have paid for a double if he planned for a grieving widow to stay with him. That will give me some leverage."

"What do you think you can do?" Eve said with a curiosity that showed she had become caught up in the detective work.

"I hope I can get a Chicago detective to get their room number and knock on their door with me. Doris Willard has got to crumble if she sees me at the door. She'll think I followed her all the way from home, and she'll assume I know a lot more than I do.

Then he snapped his fingers. "I've got an idea," he added, improvising, "You stay here and watch that bank of elevators. If they leave, follow them as best you can. I'll go and try to get a cop, and if you're not here when I get back, I'll wait for you. If you follow them someplace and want to pass on a message, call the bell captain and ask him to look for me in the lobby."

"You've got it, Dick Tracy," Eve said, smiling.

Berg walked out of the hotel and went to the first taxi waiting in line. "Is there a police precinct close?" he said, sticking his head in the open window on the passenger's front door.

"Sure. It's not too far."

"Okay," Berg said as he climbed into the back seat. "Let's go there."

The driver stopped the cab in front of an old two story red brick building that no one could mistake for anything but a police station. Not with police cars parked every which way out front. As he climbed the steps leading to the front door, Berg wondered if it was shift change time. That would explain all the police cars.

Inside, he found a glass enclosed cage, in which the desk sergeant sat, filling out forms.

"Point me to the detectives, will you?" Berg said, bending over to talk through a round hole cut in the glass.

The sergeant gestured with his thumb, pointing over his right shoulder. Berg walked around the glass cage and through a doorway. He found himself in a cavernous room, designed, it appeared, for a bigger detective squad. There were only six desks, lined up in rows of two across the middle of the room. Cream-colored paint peeled from the walls, discolored by soot. A beefy, crew-cut man of about forty-five stood up from his desk and came toward Berg, moving lightly on his feet as he weaved his way around desks.

"What can I do for you?" the man asked in a voice slightly hoarse, studying Berg with his eyes.

Berg took out his credentials case and showed it to the man, who introduced himself as John Demski. Then he quickly laid out the story of Doris Willard, ending with the fact that his wife, pressed into surveillance duty, was watching to see if Doris and what now appeared to be her lover were still in the hotel.

"What would you like us to do?" Demski asked.

"I'd like you to go with me and knock on their door. The opportunity to question them now is too good to miss."

"Nothing like catching a guy with his pants down, you mean?" Demski said, chuckling.

"Exactly. And nothing like catching a grieving widow in somebody else's bed."

"I'm game. My partner's stuck working on reports anyway."

Demski pulled his suitcoat off the back of his chair and led Berg out a door that opened onto a parking lot on the side of the building. His car was standard detective issue, plain Ford sedan with blackwall tires and old-fashioned hubcaps. When they got to the hotel, Demski parked the car next to a fireplug.

Inside they found Eve, who said Doris and Francois hadn't come back to the lobby. Demski went to the desk marked "assistant manager" and showed his badge to the woman who sat there. Berg followed along.

"I need the room number of, uh," Demski said, and then he paused and looked toward Berg.

"Francois Beloit," Berg put in.

Berg thought the assistant manager might give Demski an argument, but she didn't. Demski probably didn't have many people argue with him, he guessed.

After a few keystrokes at her computer terminal, the assistant manager looked up and said, "Four six seven." On the way to the elevator, Berg caught Eve's attention and pointed to Demski, then to himself, then straight up.

As they approached the door, Demski took out his credentials case and rapped loudly with his knuckles. In a few seconds, a male voice said through the door, "Yes, who is it?"

Demski stuck his badge in front of the peephole and replied loudly, "Chicago Police. We want to talk to you."

"Just a minute," said a shaky voice from inside.

In maybe ten seconds the door opened, and Demski, not waiting to be asked in, pushed the door open wider and walked in. Berg followed behind, noting how slickly it had all been done. Demski had merely said what he wanted, he hadn't demanded anything, and he later could testify that he took the open door as an invitation to go in.

When Doris Willard saw Berg, she gasped and shook her head from side to side, looking like she was about to break down. She was lying in the bed nearest the door, the covers pulled up to her chin. Her clothes were laid out neatly on the other bed. Berg could see that she had been wearing pink lace bikini panties and a matching bra. Hardly widow's garb, he thought, but then guessed that black wouldn't have been more appropriate.

Francois Beloit had taken the time to put his pants on before he opened the door, but Berg noticed that he hadn't zipped them up. "What do you want?" Beloit asked, his voice unsteady.

"You've got some questions to answer," Demski told him. "And you too," he added, turning to look at Doris.

"What about?" Beloit asked.

"With Chief Berg here with me," Demski said, "I think you know."

"Who is he? I've never seen either one of you before."

"Tell him who I am, Mrs. Willard," Berg suggested.

"He's from the university police," Doris said softly.

"What are you doing here?" Beloit said.

"A much better question is, what are you doing here, and what is she doing with you?" Berg countered, pointing at Doris. "But we all know the answers to those questions, don't we?"

"What business is that of yours?" Beloit replied, getting some strength in his voice.

"Don't cop an attitude with us," Demski snarled at Beloit. "You're in no position. I'd rather arrest you than look at you."

"A number of things are our business," Berg said, grateful to Demski for getting the tone back to where he wanted it. "But for now we'll stick to the big one. We figured Doris was behind her husband's murder, but until we found you, we weren't sure why. Except for the half million in insurance, of course, which you lied to me about," Berg added, raising his eyebrows while looking at Doris.

Until then Beloit had been standing. Now he sat down on the bed where his and Doris's clothes were piled.

"Tell us about the cyanide, Francois," Berg ordered, looking at Beloit and sensing weakness in him.

"What cyanide?" he asked meekly. "I don't know anything about cyanide. Doris told me the police were asking questions about Frank's death, but I don't know anything about it."

"What about you, Doris?" Berg said, turning toward her. "Don't you see that it's time to stop lying? We know everything you've done since the day Frank died. We know about Francois, we know about the insurance, and we know about how Frank was killed. You really haven't been very smart, you know."

"I don't know what to say to you," Doris said, her bottom lip quivering as she spoke. "I didn't kill Frank, and I didn't even know about the insurance."

"Bullshit," Berg countered. "We know you signed the checks to pay for it, twice a year."

A look of fear came over Doris. To Berg it looked like she felt trapped. But soon she said, "I just wrote whatever checks Frank told me to write, then he took care of stuffing the envelopes and mailing them off."

"And you never wondered what hundreds of dollars a year were going to TIAA for?"

"I knew that's who had his pension money. That's all I knew about it."

If she's lying, she's good at it, Berg thought, forced to admire what appeared to be her quick thinking.

Demski had been standing against the wall listening. He took a step toward Doris and said, "I may not be a fancy college professor like Francois here, but how dumb do I look to you? You know, most women who kill their husbands are smart enough to wait more than a week before they run off with their lover."

"Neither of you know anything about how it was," Doris said, and she began to cry softly.

Berg hoped that meant she was ready to talk.

"Tell us about it," he said gently, leaning toward her.

"I loved Frank, and I never would have done anything to hurt him. I didn't even want to divorce him. I cared about him."

"You wanted her husband out of the way, didn't you Francois?" Berg asked. "With him gone, you wouldn't have to meet in Chicago."

"I wanted her to divorce Frank. I admit that."

"And then what?" Berg said. "Are you married?"

"No, I've been divorced for two years."

"So when Doris didn't want a divorce, you thought of cyanide?"

"No. I know nothing about that."

"Where were you Friday afternoon a week ago?"

"I'm a visiting professor at the University of Minneapolis this semester. I was there."

"Do you teach on Fridays?" Berg said.

"No, but I was there nevertheless."

"So when did this get started with Francois?" Berg asked, turning again to Doris.

"About a year ago."

"Why Chicago?" Berg asked, not sure why.

"We hadn't seen each other since the semester started," Doris replied. "After Frank died, I needed to be with someone who cares about me, and I wanted to get away from the house. Chicago seemed like a good place to meet for both of us."

Berg doubted she still thought that was true. "Why did you need to get away from your house? It doesn't look like you've been missing Frank."

"You really have no idea," Doris said, crying harder now. "How do you think it makes me feel to have been cheating on him and then to have him die?"

Berg had no answer to that. He wished he had, because maybe then he'd know how good a suspect Doris Willard really was.

"Do you have anything more to do here?" Berg asked as he turned toward Demski.

"Not right now I don't."

Berg looked at Doris, who was still crying. What he couldn't tell was what her tears were for. "We'll talk more when you get back home," he said to her. Then he followed Demski out of the room.

"You've got a lot more experience than I do," Berg said as they walked toward the elevator. "What do you think?"

"Hard to tell. I always find women hard to read, so I don't guess I can help you much with her. But I wouldn't trust the Frenchman if I were you. I'll bet he either was conning us or he's been conning her."

Chapter Twelve

THE VERY FIRST THING ON MONDAY MORNING, BERG MADE A CALL TO THE CHIEF OF the University of Minneapolis police. "One of our faculty is a visiting professor at Minneapolis this semester—he's a chemist of some type, but I don't know what department he'd be in," Berg said as he straightened the items on his desk that the night cleaning crew had moved during their weekly dusting. "He's a suspect in a murder investigation, and I was hoping you'd check his alibi for us."

"Sure, we can do that," the chief said. "We've got a couple of departments where a chemist might be, but we can find him easy enough. Who is he and what do you want us to find out?"

"His name's Francois Beloit. The murder occurred here Friday the week before last, late in the afternoon. Beloit says he was in Minneapolis."

"Was he supposed to teach that day, do you know?" the chief asked.

"He told me he doesn't teach on Fridays, and I assume it's true," Berg said, falling into his habit of being more careful with details than necessary.

"What's involved in the crime, if you don't mind telling me?" the chief said.

"No problem. You ought to know. He's having an affair with the wife of a chemistry professor here. Beloit says he wanted her to get a divorce, and she says she didn't want to get one. It's a long story, but it looks like her husband was killed with cyanide, somehow delivered in a vapor or spray."

"Sounds interesting. I'll get a detective on it this morning, and we'll get back to you as soon as we have something."

An hour later, Jane Samuels came into Berg's office and dropped in a chair.

"You look beat," Berg said, looking up from the book he was reading.

"You don't know the half of it. I've been at it all weekend."

"I thought you'd like reading about spies."

"Reading is one thing. Mostly I was finding things and skimming. I checked all through the books in the university library. There's a lot of stuff there. The trouble is, it's spread out over a bunch of places and it's hard to decide where to look. They've thrown out their card catalogue, you know. You've got to look things up by computer, which is okay if you know exactly what words to type into it. Otherwise you're dead."

"Tell me about it. That's why I have to have someone else do my research."

After Jane gave Berg a dirty look, he held up his hands in surrender and said, "Don't blame me, I didn't have anything to do with computerizing everything."

"Anyway, after I finally finished at the main library, I went to the public library. Have you been down there lately?"

"No, not for three or four years."

"You're lucky. About the only people there are homeless. The woman at the desk says that they're waiting when the place opens in the morning and they stay all day. They take up most of the chairs to sleep. Plus some of them sleep in the stacks, on the floor."

"Not an easy place to do research, it sounds like," Berg put in, trying to show he appreciated the troubles she had faced.

"You said it." After pausing to sigh, Jane went on. "Anyway, it's bad all the way around. I got mad at them for being there, then mad at myself for getting mad. It's not their fault." Then another pause. "I got you a book."

"What did you find?"

"It's a book by Allen Dulles," Jane said, handing Berg the book. "You know, the former CIA director."

Berg took the book and looked at the title, *Great True Spy Stories*.

"Looks like the right genre."

"You want me to tell you the story, or do you want to read it? I took notes before I decided I should check it out for you."

"Why don't you tell me the stuff I should know. I can read it later."

"The book is a collection of stories by other people. The one you're interested in is by John Steele. It's the story of a KGB assassin named Stashinski who was sent to Germany to kill a couple of Ukrainian nationalists. Evidently they were publishing stuff that caused trouble for the Soviets back in the Ukraine. Anyway, the KGB armory provided a very special weapon. It was an aluminum cylinder about six inches long and three quarters of an inch in diameter. The book says that it was loaded with cyanide that was sealed in an ampule. When the weapon was discharged, it ejected a fine spray."

"Does the book say how the weapon was used?"

"Stashinski was told that it had an effective range of eighteen inches. He was supposed to fire it either into the victim's face, or at least hit him chest high. The face was better, because that would be more sure to startle the victim into inhaling."

"That sure sounds like what we're looking for. Anything else?"

"Professor Willard was climbing a stairway, right?"

"Yes."

"The KGB told Stashinski that's the best place to catch a victim. The idea is that you spray it in the victim's face as you're passing him on the stairway, as the victim is going up. That way, you can go right by him quickly, and since you're going down the vapors won't get you. The book says the vapors rise."

"That's what I gather. The chair of the chemistry department tells me the stuff is very volatile." Berg thought for a second and then continued, "So how well did the thing work?"

"Worked perfectly. Both of Stashinski's victims died right off. Cyanide evidently constricts all the arteries going to the brain. The KGB told Stashinski that the effects would be long gone before an autopsy could be done, so the poison would be undetectable. Here's what you'll really like. The death evidently appears to be from a heart attack."

"Good show," Berg said, smiling in delight. "Any details on how the thing was constructed?"

"No, not really."

"Does the book say how the assassin was supposed to manipulate the thing?"

"No, just that he was told to carry it in a newspaper."

Berg didn't much believe in coincidences, and he knew enough now to believe Willard had been killed by a weapon very much like the one described in the story. He also believed the killer had found out about the weapon the same way Jane Samuels had, by doing research.

As Jane hurried off to class, Berg hoped that the library could tell him that someone with a connection to Willard had checked the Dulles book out recently. Berg called the public library, got the head librarian on the phone, and told her who he was.

"I need to know who has checked out a particular book in the last couple of years. Will your records show that?"

"The records will show it, but it's against the law for me to give you the information."

Berg didn't believe it. He knew about the Buckley Amendment, which made schools restrict access to student records, and he thought that might be what the librarian was talking about. "What law is that?" Berg asked.

"I don't know what it's called, but the state legislature passed it three or four years ago. The law says it's a crime to give circulation information to anyone, including the police."

"Who in heaven's name thought that up? I've got a murder investigation going here."

"I know it sounds dumb. It happened because of a scheme the FBI had for catching spies. It involved checking who took out certain books. I think they were technical books from some university libraries. Columbia University I think was one of them. Anyway, the national association that represents librarians got excited about it, and someone talked the legislature into passing a law against it."

"Is there any way I can get the information?" Berg said.

"The law says you have to get a court order."

"Well, I guess I could get one. I'm sure the judge would sign one, but look, can you at least tell me if there is anything there worth getting an order for? I'd hate to get an order just to find out that no one has taken the book out in the last couple of years."

"Sure, I don't know why I can't do that. What's the name of the book?"

Berg provided the name, plus the call number, which he read off the spine of the book. He held for two or three minutes and then heard the librarian come back on the line.

"I can tell you that two people have checked the book out in the last two years, not counting yesterday. Before those two times, no one had taken it out for over a year."

Berg tried to think of some way to get the information he needed by asking more questions. He couldn't come up with a way to get all the information, but he did think of something.

"I hate to bother you, but could you check a little further for me? I'm interested in someone who might have been involved in the murder of a professor at the university. Could you check your membership records to see, say, what kind of people took the book out? Maybe we can still at least find that I don't need to bother with a court order."

"Okay. I'm not sure what you want me to look for, but I'll pull the records."

"I don't either," Berg said. "It's just a shot in the dark. But thanks."

Again Berg waited. He didn't mind. He didn't look forward to getting a court order. First he'd have to get someone to find the law the librarian had told him about, because it would have to be cited in the order. Then he'd have to convince someone in the district attorney's office to draft the order and take it to a judge.

"Looks to me like you're out of luck," the librarian said when she spoke again. "Almost two years ago the book was checked out by a high school student. Same thing, but a different student, about six months ago. I expect they used it to write term papers."

"Probably too smart to check the book out," Berg mumbled to himself after hanging up. Maybe there are fingerprints, though, he thought. He knew it wasn't a simple thing to get good prints off some papers, but he could give it a try. Berg picked up the phone and called Catherine Michaelman, the university police's fingerprint expert.

"Kate," he began, "do you think you can get a print off of a library book?"

"Maybe. I'd have to see the book."

"I'll be right over."

Berg considered Kate Michaelman to be the department's best detective. She had started working part-time in the department a few years before, doing clerical work while in college. Before graduating she decided to stay on, and she had made detective in record time. Sexual assaults were the most serious crime the university police faced regularly, and most of the work on those fell to her. Being a woman helped establish trust with female victims, but that was just an extra benefit. Mostly she was effective because she was a very able cop.

Kate retained the taut build of the college swimmer she had been, and Berg knew that she could hold her own with anyone. He had heard the story of one football player charged with rape who tried to avoid arrest by walking over her. The way Berg heard it, the guy didn't end up walking again until the city police helped him out of the emergency room on his way to jail a couple of hours later.

"Here it is," Berg said, handing Kate the book. "What do you think?"

"I doubt we'll get much but smudges off this kind of paper, but we'll see."

Kate got out her latent print kit and worked over the page where the story of the cyanide weapon began. As she expected, all she found were some smudges.

"What's this involved in?" she said.

While Berg was telling her the story, Kate leafed through the book. When he had finished, she pointed to the acknowledgments page in the front.

"Look here. The stories appeared first in other places. Let's see about this one." Kate checked for the title of the story Berg had shown her and found it near the end of the acknowledgments. "Here it is. It originally was published in a 1962 issue of *LIFE* magazine. They've got those in the university library."

They took Berg's Corvette to the main library. There wasn't another parking place for a quarter mile, so he parked at one of the spots in front of the loading dock, knowing no one would give him a ticket. They walked in through the back door, and Kate led him to the fourth floor stacks where bound periodicals were kept, carrying her kit.

"Here they are," Kate said, pointing to the issues of *LIFE*. She pulled the bound volume containing the right issue off the shelf, carried it to the nearest carrel, and after checking the table of contents, turned to the page where the story she was looking for began. "Let's check these pages for prints," she said. "This paper should be easy to get prints from if they aren't too old."

She carefully worked on the first page of the story, and then on all the pages that followed, finding nothing but a few faint smudges. "It looks to me like someone wiped them clean," she told Berg. "Let me check some other pages."

When she did, she found prints on the pages before and after where the story of the cyanide weapon appeared. "It sure looks like someone rubbed off the prints," she said.

As they were walking toward the library exit, Berg's pager vibrated on his belt, and he pressed the button to see the number he'd been sent. It was his secretary's. "Let's find an office where I can borrow a phone," he said to Kate.

"Follow me," she ordered. "I learned my way around every inch of this place when I was a student here."

She led Berg to a narrow stairway that joined the fourth floor stacks with the stacks on the third floor. The stairway was all metal: walls, ceiling, and steps, painted in the same gray the Navy used on its ships. Their footsteps reverberated in the stairway as if they were inside a big steel drum. The stairway also seemed to sway as they walked down it, but Berg figured that was just an illusion.

Kate led him out of the stacks on the third floor and into an office marked "Government Documents," where Berg found a librarian who let him use her phone. He dialed Irene's number and heard her answer.

"What's up?" Berg said into the phone.

"The chief of the University of Minneapolis police called. I thought you'd want to know right away."

"Absolutely," Berg said, feeling a familiar knot of anticipation form in his stomach. "What kind of news does he have?"

"He wanted me to tell you that his detective talked to Professor Beloit's chair. The chair says he knows Professor Beloit was in Minneapolis Friday afternoon, the week before last, because he had to call him at home to discuss a question about a travel expense reimbursement. The chair says he's sure about the day because it was the deadline for submitting a reimbursement request to the accounting department. He remembers his secretary telling him to call Professor Beloit at home because the following Monday would be too late."

"Okay, thanks. I'll see you later," Berg said and then put down the phone, disappointed that Beloit wasn't turning out to be a good suspect. Unless, Berg though to himself, Beloit got to his chair before we did.

Berg wondered what story Beloit could have told his chair to get him to provide an alibi, and he kicked himself for not asking the University of Minneapolis police for help sooner.

Seeing his perplexity, Kate asked what the problem was.

"One of the suspects was supposedly at the University of Minneapolis the day of the murder. The police there just checked. The information may be bad, but if it isn't, it's one suspect down."

"Why couldn't he have hired someone to do it?" Kate asked.

"I guess he could have, but I don't know how we'd prove it."

"You prove it by following the money trail," Kate told him, her voice showing her surprise that Berg hadn't thought of the obvious.

"Any ideas how to do that?" Berg asked.

"'Seek and ye shall find,'" Kate told him, smiling as she turned his divinity training back on him. "One of my friends from college is a graduate student in computer science. He's one of the best hackers there is. He can get into anyone's bank account if we want him to."

Berg was uneasy. He knew that hacking into financial records could get you into big trouble. Evidently Kate knew what was bothering him. "We won't get into any trouble. He's helped the city police and the U.S. attorney's office when I've asked him to—all illegally, of course. They can hardly come after us."

"Okay," Berg said, surprising himself at how little he was bothered by Kate's idea.

"Who is it?" she said.

"Francois Beloit. He teaches chemistry here, but this semester he's in Minneapolis."

"Let's go see if my friend can find out anything unusual about Beloit's withdrawals near the time of the murder. Last I heard, hit men want cash on delivery."

A few minutes later Kate introduced Berg to a large unshaven man named Charles Upshaw, who they had found sitting in front of a computer terminal in the computer science department. The man wore Levi's and a lumberjack's shirt that looked unwashed since the semester began. His handshake was limp and he didn't meet Berg's eyes.

As Upshaw began confidently typing away at the keyboard,

using the information Kate had given him, Berg was reminded anew that social graces don't correlate with skill.

Kate and Berg stood around watching. Berg, at least, was in awe of what he saw. Berg himself could barely use a computer for word processing. Here, he said to himself, is a guy who can play the computer like Yo Yo Ma plays the cello.

After a few false starts, which Upshaw seemed to take merely as challenges, he got first into Beloit's local records and then into an account he had at a bank in Minneapolis.

"Ah," Upshaw said. "Here's something. He took five thousand in cash from his Minneapolis bank a few days before the date you gave me."

"Check both accounts for a couple of years. Let's see if he's done it before," Kate told him.

After two minutes Upshaw had an answer. "Nothing special that I can see," Upshaw told Kate, ignoring Berg.

Walking away from Upshaw, Berg was elated. "That sounds like the right price for a killing, and I can't imagine a legitimate purpose for taking out so much cash."

"Not when plastic buys anything," Kate said.

"I screwed up in not getting the University of Minneapolis police to check out his alibi right away," he said ruefully. "I'll have to call their chief again—or maybe this time I'll call his chair myself."

"Couldn't hurt," Kate said.

Chapter Thirteen

FRIDAY AFTERNOON, TEN DAYS EARLIER, SOMEONE CARRYING A NEWSPAPER HAD waited patiently for the chemistry department's weekly curriculum committee meeting to break up. That was not a hardship because the person had patience in large supply.

The meeting always ended at about a quarter to three, so it wasn't difficult to check once or twice by walking past the conference room on the fifth floor and glancing through the partially open doorway. When, on the second pass by the door, committee members began getting up from their chairs, it was time to go up the stairs to the sixth floor and stand outside the stairwell. From there it was possible to look through the small window in the door and see when someone was climbing the stairs from below.

The person with the newspaper did not want to be seen waiting by the door, but the risk was not great. The stairwell was at the end of the building and couldn't be seen by anyone unless they were in the short hallway outside the door.

Besides going to the stairwell, the only reason to be in that hallway was to go either to the custodian's closet or to the storeroom that were there, or to go between the long hallways that ran along each side of the sixth floor. Since there were three other crossover hallways on the floor, few people needed to come to the stairwell end of the building just to cross over, and, for going between floors, most people used the elevators at the other end of the building.

The newspaper was held chest high, so that if anyone came near the stairwell, they would apparently only see someone taking a quick look at the paper. If that happened, the plan would be abandoned for the day.

But that didn't happen. As planned, Frank Willard walked into the stairwell before anyone appeared in the sixth floor hallway, and, in a few seconds, he stepped onto the landing between the floors. That was the killer's cue to open the sixth floor stairwell door and start down the stairs.

Willard looked up, and they exchanged greetings. Then, as they were about to meet on the stairs, the killer swung the newspaper toward Willard's face and discharged the weapon hidden inside.

As soon as the weapon fired, Willard gasped in reflex action to the spray that had been blown in his face. As the killer's feet hit the fifth floor landing, Willard began to fall. Still carrying the newspaper, Willard's killer continued down the stairwell to the first floor and walked out into the first floor hallway, having met no one during the transit down the six flights of stairs.

The killer had walked quickly down the stairs, but at a pace calculated to be just slower than would be memorable to anyone.

Upon reaching the first floor hallway, there was no longer any reason for extra speed.

Once outside the building, the killer relaxed. Everything had gone off without a problem. No one had seen anything to cause suspicion and the preparations had left no trail. Only one thing remained to be done.

The killer drove away from campus and then out of the city and onto the interstate. At the first rest stop, which was fifteen miles down the road, the killer parked at the near end of the lot, a few spaces from the closest car.

Taking the newspaper in hand, the killer twisted it over and over, moving it across the five inch tube that remained inside. Even though confident that the tube would never find its way into the hands of the police, it was best to remove fingerprints.

The tube was dropped from the newspaper into a small draw-string-top trash bag that was held open with facial tissue to prevent fingerprints. The newspaper was maneuvered around the trash bag, so that both could be carried in one hand without touching the bag, and they went into the dumpster that the highway department kept at the rest area. The trash bag was dropped in one corner and the newspaper tossed on top of other trash.

After getting a drink of water at the comfort station, the killer drove out of the rest area and, after turning around at the next exit, headed back into the city.

As the killer drove, the adrenaline that had started pumping three quarters of an hour before was still working, still overactive, and this forced a mental reliving of the events that had led up to that moment.

The idea from the beginning had been to find a way to dispose of Willard without his death raising suspicion. Willard's death should be attributed to natural causes, and that had taken some doing.

The first step was to find a path someone else had traveled successfully. There was no sense in reinventing anything, the killer knew, and it was also impossible to think of everything the first time through. The killer was used to university life, so looking for books and articles in the university library seemed the best starting point.

What was needed was a poison that was hard to detect and a delivery system that could be used with relative safety. Since everyone knew Willard had a bad heart, the best hope was something that would mimic a heart attack. It took the better part of two days, but diligent searching finally turned up the story by John Steele, "Assassin Disarmed by Love," in *LIFE* magazine.

There was one main problem with the story, though—it didn't tell how the weapon described in the story actually worked. But, that problem could be gotten around by a little reverse engineering since all that would be needed was a mechanism for crushing an ampule and for spraying out the cyanide.

With a little thought, a solution came quickly to mind. All one had to do was glue a glass ampule into the end of a tube. Behind it could be put a small cylinder of compressed air, the kind used in a darkroom to blow dust off photo negatives. If rigged right, pushing the compressed air cylinder into the ampule would break the ampule and at the same time push in on the plunger at the top of the cylinder, releasing compressed air.

A defect in the engineering immediately presented itself, however. An endcap would be needed to stop the crushed ampule from being pushed out the front of the tube. Perhaps an endcap with a lot of little holes drilled in it would be needed Or maybe a piece of tough window screen would work, the killer thought.

Securing the compressed air cylinder entailed a little risk, but the risk was manageable. The killer went to a supply store for professional photographers. The place was in a low-rent district and was more warehouse than store, which worked well for the typical customer who didn't care how the merchandise was displayed. The layout also worked well for someone who didn't want to be remembered as having bought a compressed air cylinder.

The killer went around the store picking up inexpensive but bulky items, and also the small compressed air cylinder. When out of anyone's sight, the cylinder went into a jacket pocket. The killer knew the chance of being caught was minimal, and if caught, sticking the cylinder into a pocket could probably be explained away, at least enough to avoid arrest, as an absentminded mistake.

Getting the cyanide and putting it in an ampule was easy for someone with access to the chemistry department's storeroom, since both cyanide and unsealed ampules were kept there. All that was needed was a few minutes to work unobserved. Graduate students worked at night, so coming in late wasn't the answer.

No one was ever around early in the morning, however, so going in at six one morning provided the needed privacy. The killer simply took from the storeroom a bottle of cyanide and an unsealed one milliliter ampule of the type used for smelling salts, and then filled and sealed the ampule in a fume hood. The cyanide was back in the storeroom within five minutes.

The killer had planned to use a piece of electrical conduit for the tube of the weapon, but by chance hit upon something better. There was an old TV antenna in the killer's basement, put there when cable came into the neighborhood. The mast, it turned out, had an inside diameter of about one and three-eighths inches, and the stolen compressed air cylinder fit inside with only a small gap.

A snug fit was easily obtained, one that would keep it from falling out but not from being pushed easily, by wrapping the cylinder with black friction tape. By taking into account the length of the compressed air cylinder and the diameter of the cyanide ampule, it was easily determined that a five-inch piece of the antenna mast was needed. This was cut off with a hacksaw.

The plastic endpiece was pulled off the plunger of the compressed air cylinder, so all that remained was a small plastic tube sticking out the end of the cylinder. A one-and-three-eighths-inch disk was cut out of plastic, and a hole drilled in the center. The plastic tube from the compressed air cylinder was then fitted into this hole, and the two pieces glued together.

The plunger disk thus created would serve as a miniature battering ram at the end of the compressed air cylinder. When the time came to push the cylinder farther up the tube, the disk would crush the cyanide ampule and through the hole in the center would come a blast of air that would spray the cyanide out the front of the weapon.

So as to get a good seal between the plunger disk and the tube, a bead of silicone was applied to the outside of the disk, letting the silicone hang over the edge slightly. By a small amount of shaving with a razor knife after the silicone dried, it was possible to get a fit as good as between the tube and plunger in a bicycle tire pump.

Now an endcap was needed for the five-inch tube. The best material at hand was aluminum screening, which was easily obtained by taking a screen from one of the windows in the house that never was opened anyway. From this the killer cut a disk two inches in diameter. Working carefully, the screen was wired tautly over the end of the five-inch tube and then further secured by epoxy resin.

The last step was to glue the cyanide ampule into the end of the tube, just behind the screen. This was done by placing the tube on a table protected by newspaper, screen end down, carefully lowering in the ampule, and then, with a stiff artist's brush, applying epoxy resin all around the ampule to hold it in place.

When the resin dried, the killer wiped everything clean of fingerprints, put on a pair of latex examination gloves to guard against new ones, and inserted the cylinder into the five inch tube, taking care to work the silicone just enough to fit the plunger disk into the tube. The bottom of the compressed air cylinder was then even with the back of the tube, and the plunger disk almost touched the cyanide ampule.

Chapter Fourteen

"DO YOU WANT TO STAY ON THIS CASE?" BERG SAID TO KATE MICHAELMAN AS THEY walked out of the computer science department on Monday morning.

"Sure, why not? It should be interesting."

"It's interesting, all right. The problem is, it's too interesting. I really don't have any idea what to do now."

"You need to drop me off at the department, anyway. Why don't you come in and we can talk about it?"

"Good idea," Berg said, knowing he needed all the help he could get. He began to tell her the rest of what he knew about the case on the drive to Kate's office and finished the story while sitting in his car in the parking lot.

Once inside the police building, Berg and Kate went to her office. It was barely large enough for her battered wooden desk—which reminded Berg of the desks his high school teachers had sat behind in study hall—and two inexpensive chairs. She had decorated the walls with stills from 1960s movies, bordered in polished aluminum frames.

"So the suspects you've got are Willard's wife and her lover, mainly, and then Lerner and the secretary who found the body, right?" she began.

"That's it. Lerner and the secretary I have no idea what to do with now. And Beloit's supposedly got an alibi—which I'll check more on—but that doesn't make much difference if he used his five thousand in cash to have someone kill Willard for him. I just don't know what real evidence we've got against him or Willard's wife."

After pausing to think, Berg went on, continuing to think out loud. "There is the life insurance angle, of course, especially if we put that together with the love interest. I don't know, though. The affair may or may not have been a motive to kill Willard."

"Why don't you check on Beloit now?" Kate suggested. "I think your idea of calling his department chair was the best one. You can use my phone."

Berg was happy to follow Kate's lead. He moved to her desk chair and called the University of Minneapolis. The operator was able to tell him what department Beloit was in and the name of the chair. Berg asked to be connected. Kate leaned close to hear both sides of the conversation. After a secretary answered, Berg was able to get the department chair on the line.

After identifying himself, he began, "You remember being asked about the whereabouts of Francois Beloit on a certain day?"

"Yes, a detective stopped by."

"Let me level with you. I'm calling direct because I don't want to see you get in trouble for trying to help a friend. I don't know what he told you, but Professor Beloit is a murder suspect, and we have good evidence that he was here the day you said he was in Minneapolis. I've got to warn you that lying to the police about this can get you sent to prison as an accessory after the fact."

Berg let what he had said hang in the air for a couple of seconds before going on. "Now's the time to come clean on this. If you do, I'll forget what you told the detective earlier. If you don't, I'm calling the Minneapolis district attorney's office as soon as we get off the phone."

"Damn Francois," the chair said, sounding like he had been both frightened and relieved. He took Berg up on his offer, without knowing that most of what Berg had told him was a bluff. "He called me at home on a Sunday all worked up," the chair began. "He said the police were suspicious about his possible involvement in a murder hundreds of miles away simply because he couldn't prove where he had been on a particular Friday. Because I know he's in his lab about all the time—in fact I don't know of his going anywhere this semester—I agreed to help.

"Why'd you do that?" Berg said.

"I don't really know, but I can tell you this, I never would have helped him if I thought he was involved in a murder. Frankly the idea of Francois killing anybody struck me as ludicrous."

"Why's that?" Berg said, curious because he knew that, given the right circumstances, any kind of person could commit murder.

"I guess because he seems like a twerp to me."

"Regrettably, twerps do their share of killing," Berg said. "But I see your point. Anyway, believe me, you've done yourself a big favor."

With obvious relief in his voice, the chair asked, "Do you think you can keep from telling Francois that I've backed off what I said earlier?"

"Probably," Berg said. "I'll do my best."

"Good going," Kate said, smiling, when Berg hung up the phone. "That changes the picture."

"It does," Berg agreed. "But I still don't know where to go with what we've got. If we confront Beloit, he'll just continue to swear he was home the Friday Willard was killed—though I don't know how he'd explain the five thousand dollars. I suppose I could call and surprise him with it, and see what that shakes loose."

"We've got a problem there," Kate said, her voice showing concern, "since we got the information illegally."

"You're right. Let's hold what we've got for now and see if we can find a way to do something with it later."

"I wish we could find out if Doris Willard knew about her husband's insurance," Kate put in. "Her explanation of just writing the checks that Willard told her to, and thinking checks to TIAA were for his pension—who knows? Could be true, but I don't see anyway to find out. I doubt a husband's life insurance is something a wife talks much about with other people."

"I still think the biggest thing against Doris Willard is her pushing for a quick cremation," Berg said. "But I don't know where we can go with that either. The reason she gave me sounded plausible enough, but I wish I'd been smart enough to take you with me when I interviewed her. I couldn't tell what to make of her, and now that I've put her on her guard, going back again isn't likely to get us anywhere." Berg wasn't about to explain that it was mostly his hormones that kept him from telling what to make of her.

"I don't think we should talk to her again unless we can find something new to confront her with. Also, I don't know if you've thought of this, but from what you told me about the *LIFE* magazine story, rushing the cremation doesn't fit the scheme."

"What are you thinking of?" Berg asked with a perplexed look on his face.

"According to the story, the poison wasn't supposed to be detectable. If Willard's wife were following the script, presumably she wouldn't be too concerned about an autopsy."

"Seems right," Berg said. "But I can't believe an autopsy wouldn't find cyanide poisoning if the M.E. knew what to look for. I'll bet the real benefit of the scheme, especially with Willard, is that the death would look like a heart attack. If that idea got sold, no one would check for poison. Maybe Doris Willard knew enough not to trust the poison to be undetectable if the M.E. looked for it."

"Probably you're right," Kate said. Then, after a moment's thought, she went on, "I think it's very possible that she expected that the M.E. would see the body and think heart attack, but that when the opportunity presented itself to order a quick cremation, it was too good a chance to pass up."

"It would have been the smart thing to do."

After having pushed Berg here and there, and obviously not being impressed with some of his work, Kate gave him a little credit. "Absolutely," she said. "If the labcoat hadn't been saved, and if you hadn't thought to have the crime lab check it, she'd have been home-free for sure."

"Trouble is," Berg added, "it looks like she's going to be home-free anyway, if she did it. And Beloit with her. They can both just laugh in our faces. And maybe they should," Berg added in exasperation. "We just don't have enough on either one of them to do anything with."

"What can we do to develop another suspect?" Kate asked.

Berg thought for a moment. "I don't know. I've come up empty."

"One thing we can do," Kate said, seemingly in desperation, "in fact the only thing we may be able to do, is wait to see if a suspect shows his or her hand in some way, although I don't know what way that might be. Or we may just have to wait to see if anything else happens that we can tie in with Willard's murder."

"That's what we may be left with. But I hate to sit and wait," Berg said, feeling annoyed.

Kate brought her hands together in front of her chest, with the fingertips of one hand placed against those of the other, and she rocked her body back in her chair as she cast her eyes up toward the ceiling. Berg kept quiet while she thought out the problem.

"It didn't occur to me until now," she said, "but there is one other thing we can do. We can look backward rather than wait to look forward. It's possible Willard's murder is part of a chain, but not the first link."

"How do you propose we do that?" Berg said, intrigued.

"I don't know. I told you I only just now thought of it. We could look through our police reports, but that would be too tedious."

"They wouldn't tell us enough anyway," Berg said. "Our reports only show crimes on campus."

"The best thing I can think of is the *Weekly Observer.* But it's mostly for official information and PR, so it doesn't cover things the university would like to keep quiet. It does report some deaths of faculty, though, and some other things that might be of interest. It would be a start."

"So shall we go back to the library?"

"No," Kate said, shaking her head. "Why don't we go over to the public affairs office. They must have all the back issues, and their conference room will be more comfortable than the library."

When they walked into the conference room a few minutes later, Berg saw that Kate had been right. The room had a walnut table that seated sixteen in walnut and black leather chairs. The walls were covered in light tan grasscloth, with more walnut, this time wainscoting, below the chair rail. For decoration, there were original nineteenth century English country prints.

Though Berg had never been to the public affairs office, he thought he should have known what to expect. The university was always willing to spend money on anything the public could see. Berg never understood why. It seemed to him that the university would be better off looking like it needed money. The public affairs conference room made it seem like the university had money it could give away. On the other hand, Berg decided, since the university administration raised enormous amounts of money, they obviously knew how to do it, and, so long as they didn't tell him how to do his job, he figured he'd leave theirs to them.

Berg and Kate sat at the conference table and started going over past *Weekly Observer* issues. They decided to go back a year. One of the secretaries got them sandwiches from the faculty dining room, and they worked through lunch.

As Berg sat eating a grilled cheese sandwich and supposedly looking only at the *Weekly Observer*, he found himself distracted by Kate. She sat at the end of the table and he at the first chair on one side, so they could easily share the newspapers piled in front of them. Berg had always found Kate pretty, with her short brown hair and cute, turned-up nose. Now he thought to himself that she was beautiful. Her clothes were not provocative in the ordinary sense, just becoming—light gray wool pullover sweater, white blouse underneath, and a darker gray wool skirt—but he found them provocative nevertheless.

At the end of their search, completed more by Kate than by Berg, they found two deaths of professors in the College of Science that they thought offered some hope of developing into a lead—one death by heart attack of a fifty-one year old physics professor and one by unspecified causes of a chemistry professor, who was forty-three.

"I have a faculty meeting I have to get to at one o'clock," Berg said. "Why don't you see what you can find out about those deaths, and we can talk later."

"Okay. But tell me the truth, Eric. Aren't you going to the meeting just to avoid doing some honest work?"

"If you'd ever been to a faculty meeting you wouldn't accuse me that way," Berg assured her "It's meetings and exam grading they have to pay us for. The teaching and writing we'd do for free."

THE DIVINITY SCHOOL DIDN'T HAVE A CONFERENCE ROOM, SO THE faculty met in one of the classrooms. There was a desk in the front of the room where the dean sat, with seats occupied by Berg and his colleagues arranged in circular tiers facing him. On the walls were oil portraits of somber-looking men, all former deans of the school dating from the middle of the last century.

The last dean had resigned the year before, and a permanent replacement had not been found. So the school dragged itself along under an interim dean, a professor of New Testament whose sole distinction, besides seniority, was that he was equally disliked by everyone. Berg walked through the door as the meeting was about to begin and sat in his usual place along the side.

The only item on the agenda was the approval of new courses requested by faculty members and recommended by the curriculum committee. Never in the history of the school had the faculty failed to approve such a course—because in the unwritten rules of academe that simply wasn't done—so Berg thought the meeting would be short and painless. He knew he was wrong when the dean said he wanted to discuss a financial matter before taking up new courses.

The dean began to talk about the school's money problems. It had finished the last year over budget, he said, and this year had started out no better. The problem, according to the dean, was that the faculty was spending too much money on travel, photocopies, telephone calls, and so on, and they had to cut back. Everyone in the room, except perhaps the dean, knew that the problem was not too much spending, but the dean's inability to gather in enough donations.

As the dean droned on, the faculty began to get restive. Someone on one side of the room let out a groan. That groan was probably spontaneous, but as other faculty chuckled, somebody on the other side couldn't resist groaning himself, out of which came laughter.

The dean was so engrossed in his lecture about wasteful spending that at first he didn't seem to know what was happening. But when he heard the second groan he looked up, confused, and then, catching on, he turned his head slowly from side to side, scowling.

All of which prompted Berg, who had laughed himself, to recall the response of an old priest, who when asked what he had learned from hearing confessions for a half century, said, "There aren't any grown-up people."

After Berg walked back to his office when the meeting finally broke up, he called his wife, as he often did when he wanted to vent steam. "All interim deans aren't ineffective ignoramuses, are they?" he asked.

"No," Eve said. "Just yours. My interim dean is great, but then she's a woman."

Until then Berg had forgotten that the last dean of the College of Science, Stuart Ellingham, had been murdered on an out-of-town trip five months before.

Chapter Fifiteen

BERG KICKED HIMSELF FOR NOT THINKING OF STUART ELLINGHAM'S KILLING earlier, when he and Kate were looking for a possible connection to the Willard murder. But at that point he wasn't trying to think of a tie-in, he was looking for one in the *Weekly Observer*. It wasn't surprising that neither he nor Kate came across a reference to Ellingham's murder in the university paper. The murder was the kind of thing the university didn't want to publicize. And the local papers hadn't done more than put out an initial, sketchy report, because the murder had happened in Cincinnati, where Ellingham had attended a meeting.

Soon after Berg hung up the telephone, Mary Abbott, one of the senior professors on the faculty, came into Berg's office and sat down. The two had been friends for years, starting when Abbott was on the committee that had recruited Berg and lured him away from other schools that wanted to hire him. Abbott raised her eyebrows, creating a multitude of lines in her forehead, and leaned toward Berg. "What did you think of that show in the faculty meeting?" she asked.

"Which show," Berg said. "The dean's or our's?"

"The dean's."

"Pretty bad. I was hoping for a quick meeting too."

"Whoever groaned first groaned for all of us," she said. "The guy is insufferable. I mean that literally. I don't think we can stand to have him continue much longer. It's bad enough that he can't do anything else right, but we've got to have someone who can raise money."

"So where is your search for a new dean going?" Berg said, knowing that she was the chair of the dean search committee.

"The provost wanted us to find an outside dean, but we haven't been able to get anyone first-rate. Our latest prospect just told us that she's decided to stay where she is."

"Where does that leave us?" Berg said, disappointed that yet another promising candidate hadn't worked out.

Abbott smiled and looked closely at Berg. "It leaves me here talking to you," she said. "Over the last couple of days, I've discussed this with the other members of the committee, and we'd back you for dean if you'd do it. You could take over at the beginning of the second semester."

Berg knew that with the committee's support, the provost would probably go along, especially since the search for a new dean had already taken months longer than anybody had planned.

"I'm flattered that you asked," he said, "but I don't know. Let me think about it."

"Fair enough, but don't wait too long. We either need a new dean or I need a lobotomy."

After Abbott left, Berg sat for a few minutes and looked out the window, daydreaming about the prospect of being dean. There were benefits to it. More money for one thing, and honor. As his eyes wandered over the scene outside his window, movement at the base of the nearest tree caused him to look up in time to see a squirrel scamper up the trunk and run far out on a high limb, his teeth clamped around a big nut.

As Berg watched the squirrel, the phrase, "going the wrong way," came into his mind, and he wondered why the squirrel was taking a nut up the tree instead of burying it as he thought squirrels were supposed to do in the fall. And then the silly thought crossed his mind that maybe the squirrel was trying to tell him something.

Berg shook his head, trying to throw off the idea that a squirrel was communicating with him, and then he picked up the phone to call Kate.

"Have you come up with anything on those deaths?"

"They aren't going to lead anywhere," Kate told him. "The cause of the chemistry professor's death turned out to be simple enough. It was AIDS. I was able to get that right away from the department's secretary. It took a little longer to verify the heart attack that killed the guy from physics. Finally I got the bright idea to call the M.E.'s office. Next time, I'll start with them. It turns out they did an autopsy. The clerk pulled the report and it showed big time heart damage."

"Good work, anyway," Berg said, then paused before he switched gears. "My wife reminded me of something that might be a lead. Do you remember the science dean getting murdered when he was on a trip to Cincinnati? It was some months ago."

"I remember hearing about it at the time. I got the idea from the TV news report that there was something sleazy involved with it. He was killed in his hotel room, I think."

"That's about all I remember too. It doesn't sound like a very likely connection with the Willard murder, but it's something to look at anyway. I'll do some checking and see what I can find out."

Berg didn't have a good idea of who at the university to call for more information, so he decided to go to the best source he could think of, the Cincinnati police department's homicide division. The sergeant who answered Berg's call looked up the case number, using Ellingham's name, and found the name of the detective who had handled the case. The sergeant promised to have the detective call when he came back to the division.

Berg should have begun to prepare for his three o'clock class, but his thoughts turned back to the deanship.

"Dean Berg," he said to himself, just to see how it sounded. It sounded good, he thought. The problem was, he asked himself, how would it sound when it was "Dean Berg this," and "Dean Berg that," coming from everybody until they drove him crazy?

Soon the telephone rang. Irene answered it and told Berg that a Detective Bill Clampton was returning his call.

"Hello, thanks for calling back," Berg said into the receiver.

"No problem. You're interested in the Ellingham case, I understand."

"Yes, that's right," Berg said, hoping this lead would go somewhere sure.

"It's been a tough one. Not a lot to go on. Can I ask why you're interested?"

"Sure. We had a murder here ten days ago. Very slick cyanide poisoning of a science professor that was made to look like a heart attack. We're trying to check anything that may tie in with it."

"You'd be able to tell better than I would about a tie-in," the detective began, "but here's basically what we've got. Ellingham doesn't check out from his hotel when he's supposed to on Saturday. There's a Do Not Disturb sign on the door, but in the afternoon the maid knocks on the door and then opens it up anyway to check on the room. She finds Ellingham dead."

"What hotel is that?"

"The Hilton. Downtown. Anyway, we get there and find that he's been shot five times. Two in the head and three in the groin. The weapon was a .22. We've got the bullets, hollowpoints. We were able to get decent ballistics on some of them. From the lands and grooves, the lab says they came from a Ruger Mark II."

"Do you have the casings?" Berg said.

"No, it looks like the killer picked them up."

"What time did it happen, from what you could tell?"

"The coroner says sometime Friday night, he thinks before midnight. It was bad timing for us. Most of the people on the floor were there for the same meeting Ellingham was, and they checked out Saturday morning. We tracked some of them down the best we could. Evidently no one saw or heard anything."

"A .22 isn't very loud, but you'd think the people next door would have heard something."

"The room on one side was empty. We did reach the people on the other side, though. Depending on when it happened, they may or may not have been in the room. Also, they had their TV on some of the time."

"Any prints?"

"We went ahead and took some, but who knows what you've got in a hotel room. If we ever get a suspect we may be able to find a matching print, but I wouldn't hold out much hope."

"What's your theory?" Berg asked, thinking that he hadn't heard anything yet that would help develop a theory.

"Well, we found some other things that put a particular cast on it. Ellingham was fully dressed, shirt and pants, but there was a condom on the night stand. Laid nice and neat on top of a piece of tissue paper. Wrapper was nowhere to be found. We did, however, find a piece of a tampon wrapper on the bathroom floor. Putting all that together with the three shots in the groin, it looks like a sexual killing."

"Yes, sure does. Any prints on the tampon wrapper?"

"No, we tried to get some but weren't successful."

"Did you find any other condoms in Ellingham's room?"

"No. The best theory we've got is that a hooker brought the condom we found. They carry their own these days, you know. We think there may have been a hassle over the hooker having a period and trying to sell sex."

"What about money, credit cards, jewelry? Was that taken?"

"No. We thought that was a little strange. You'd think most hookers would at least take the cash. But maybe she got flustered after the murder."

"Do you know what meeting Ellingham was there for?"

"I've got that here somewhere." There was a shuffling of papers, and then the detective said, "Here it is. Society of Inorganic Chemists."

Chapter Sixteen

ELLINGHAM'S MURDER DID SOUND TO BERG LIKE A KILLING BY A PROSTITUTE, AS the Cincinnati police believed, but if he kept to the plan of trying to see if there was a tie-in between the Willard and Ellingham murders, Berg thought he might reach another conclusion.

If the killings were connected, Berg thought, Ellingham obviously wasn't murdered on the spur of the moment by a Cincinnati hooker. Also, if they were connected, it was hard for him to believe that Ellingham's killing was sexual at all. It was possible that both men were killed by the same jilted lover, or for some other reason that linked the men together in a sexual web, but Berg doubted it. Willard's killer had gone to great lengths to make his death seem to be something it wasn't. So, Berg reasoned, if the same person had killed Ellingham five months before, he or she probably would have tried the same trick then.

Especially when examined through that lens, there were some things about Ellingham's killing that didn't fit with it being done by a prostitute. The Cincinnati police thought the killer didn't take Ellingham's cash because she was flustered. If so, it seemed strange to Berg that she was cool enough to pick up five shell casings. He knew from having chased after shell casings himself that the killer almost certainly had to do some looking to find all five. Also, he knew too much about guns to believe many Cincinnati hookers carried Ruger Mark II's. The gun was great for targets. It certainly wasn't a purse gun.

And then, too, Berg thought, it was a little too coincidental that Ellingham was murdered at a meeting of inorganic chemists. With the chemistry tie-in, he decided he had better talk again with the chair of the chemistry department.

"Hello, Jim," Berg began when Lerner picked up the phone. "I'd like to come talk to you about Stuart Ellingham's murder. I've got some training I have to give at the police department, but could we get together around a quarter to five?"

"Sure. I don't know much about it, though."

"That's all right," Berg assured him. "I've got good information on the murder itself from the Cincinnati police. What I'm looking for is a possible connection with Willard's murder."

"I'd never thought of that before."

"I didn't either until today. Look, will you do this for me? Think about who you know who would have had a motive to kill both Willard and Ellingham. Any kind of motive. Revenge, gain, whatever. Sexual even."

"Tell me," Berg began, when after class he was seated in Lerner's office for their meeting, "what was Ellingham doing at a meeting of inorganic chemists? I thought he was a physicist."

"He was. He went to the meeting to receive an award for his support of chemical research."

"Was it announced ahead of time that he would be getting the award?"

"It was mentioned in the brochure announcing the meeting. You know how those things work. The society sends out the brochure several weeks before the meeting, listing the events. Some societies keep awards secret, but not this one."

"Did many people from your department go to the meeting?"

"Absolutely. Just about every inorganic chemist we've got. I went myself."

"So what do you think? Do we have anybody with a motive for killing Willard and Ellingham?"

"I really have trouble thinking about it that way. I don't see anyone here being a killer. I can't picture anyone here shooting or poisoning someone."

"That's probably what Abel said about Cain," Berg told him. "But you don't have to think about it that way. It's certainly possible these murders were done by a confederate. I just want your help in figuring out motives."

"Well," Lerner said slowly, "the best I can come up with is an assistant professor who was turned down for tenure last year. Willard was the chair of his tenure committee. The committee voted against tenure, and everyone knew it was Willard who was out to kill his chances. The department voted for tenure anyway, but Stuart Ellingham had the final say as a practical matter. He refused to approve tenure with a committee vote against."

"Why was Willard against him, do you know?"

"A paper the professor wrote got a bad evaluation from an outside reviewer, and that was enough for Willard. Some people are like that."

"Yes, I know," Berg said, frowning. In meetings to decide tenure, he had always argued that nobody's career should turn on a review or two, because the best work often is controversial and because reviewers sometimes get riled when they think their own work is being challenged by an upstart. "Didn't you have a say?" Berg asked.

"I recommended tenure, even argued for it. But I wasn't surprised that he turned it down. He didn't like tenure files that had blemishes, and the adverse committee vote was a blemish."

"But based on one bad evaluation," Berg said.

"True."

"What's this assistant professor's name?"

"William Appleton."

"And Appleton took it especially hard?"

"I guess I'd say that. I don't know if anyone ever takes it any way but hard, but this one was especially hard because he came close. I think it's probably easier emotionally if you get the idea over a few years that you aren't going to make it."

Berg thought Lerner was right about that. "Is Appleton here in his terminal year?" Berg said.

"Yes, and it's a mess. I believe in letting a professor have a chance to find a new job, but it never works out well."

Berg knew what Lerner meant. He'd seen the same thing happen. Terminal years were always a problem.

"Had Appleton made any threats?" Berg asked.

"No, nothing like that. I've talked to him, and he thinks he got a raw deal, but he never has made any threats."

Berg knew that question hadn't helped much because if someone wanted revenge and were smart, they wouldn't make threats.

"The question is, I guess," Berg said, "would Appleton have wanted revenge?"

"I guess so, but that doesn't mean I think he killed anybody."

"I know. You don't need to keep telling me that. But look," Berg said, switching gears, "that reminds me of something. You heard that the Cincinnati police believe Ellingham was killed by a prostitute?"

"Yes, I'd heard that."

"How likely do you think that was?"

"Not likely at all. Do you know why they thought that?"

"They told me, but I better not pass it on. I can tell you this, though. Their theory is based on good evidence. The question is, was the evidence planted?"

Then, thinking Lerner might be able to help if he had more facts, Berg decided to give some to him, even if he was a suspect. Berg didn't see how it could hurt, because if Lerner had killed Ellingham, Berg wouldn't be telling him anything he didn't already know.

"Let me tell you one thing. The way the police read the evidence, Ellingham may have been killed because he got into an argument with a hooker who was trying to sell sex while having her period. You knew Ellingham. Do you think that washes?"

Lerner didn't hesitate. "No way," he said, waving his arm dismissively. "First, I don't see Stuart fooling around with a prostitute. I've never thought that from the first time I heard the rumor. But even if he would hire a prostitute, I don't see him doing it in the hotel where the meeting is going on. If someone saw her go into his room, the story would start flying immediately."

"That's an angle I hadn't considered," Berg said, sorry to have missed what seemed an obvious point. "What about the argument part of the theory?"

"That doesn't sound like Stuart either. He was a very gentle, polite man. I think he'd have been more likely to apologize to the woman and pay her anyway if he didn't want to go ahead with sex. I really don't see him doing anything to get a prostitute mad enough to kill him."

Berg tried to read Lerner as he spoke, and he wondered why, if Lerner were the killer, would he try so hard to shoot down the police's theory. Maybe, Berg decided, because Lerner was a very slick customer who knew that he had to throw Berg off at all cost.

"Well, that takes us back to where we started," Berg began again. "If a hooker didn't kill him, someone else did, and I'll bet it was someone from here. Anyone else you can think of who had a motive?"

"When you called you said any motive. Revenge, gain, sex, whatever. There is one person who gained from both deaths. I can't think of anyone with a sexual motive. And," he went on, holding up his hands as if to stop Berg, "before you ask, no, I don't think Stuart Ellingham was mixed up with Janet Miller. That is something I really can't picture."

"So tell me about the person who gained."

"His name's Jerry Duncan—Gerald Duncan. He's one of the inside candidates to replace Ellingham as dean of the College of Science, pretty clearly the leading inside candidate. He's young for his standing in his field, only about forty. He's a first-rate chemist. Remember I told you that Frank Willard was a contender for a prize for excellence in research?"

"Yes, I remember."

"Jerry Duncan is the other contender."

"You think he might kill someone for a prize?" Berg asked, knowing immediately what a stupid question it was. He knew very well that some people would kill for anything, others for nothing.

"No, I don't think he would kill for a prize. I don't think Jerry would kill anybody. But, as a matter of fact, it isn't just the prize we're talking about," Lerner began to explain, bristling at what Berg had said. "The prize is the major prize in the College of Science. It's given once a year to a professor in the college. By tradition, the prize is rotated around the departments, not necessarily one year to each department. We all fight over whose department should be the one for a particular year. Anyway, this year is our year. If Jerry gets it, it will strengthen his position for the deanship."

"Very much, do you think?"

"Yes, I'd say so. I'm not saying it would make the difference, but it would give him very helpful recognition in other departments in the college. The outside candidate for the deanship is strong though."

"How is it decided who gets the prize?" Berg said.

"The chair of the department decides. In this case, me."

"What does your faculty think about not having a say?" Berg asked, knowing that faculty governance was one of the hottest buttons in the university.

"They don't much like it," Lerner allowed, "but some things are best decided by those above the fray."

Berg left it at that, mostly because he agreed. "It so happens that I know Duncan, but just a little. What kind of guy is he?"

"Like I told you, first-rate chemist. Works very hard. Also, very tuned-in to campus politics. I think everyone around here expected that he would want to be dean someday. He's been making the right moves for as long as he's been here."

"Do I assume you don't think Doris Willard had any motive to see Stuart Ellingham dead?"

"I don't think she had any motive to see either Stuart or Frank dead."

"No chance she and Gerald Duncan were involved?" Berg asked, trying to cover all the possibilities he could think of. If she was fooling around with one of her husband's colleagues, he thought, maybe she'd been doing it with another.

"That would really be stretching. Frankly, Jerry doesn't take much time for women. You see him with a woman sometimes, from time to time in fact with Marilyn Harris—you know, the secretary who found Willard's body. But he's here working most of the time."

"Were things serious between Duncan and Marilyn Harris?" Berg asked, suddenly more interested in the conversation.

"Not that I could see. Marilyn dated a few professors and graduate students, but nothing that amounted to anything so far as I could tell."

Hearing about Marilyn Harris reminded Berg of a loose end he had been meaning to tie up.

"Did you ever find the books Willard had with him on the stairs?"

"No. We hit a wall on that. I had my secretary look all over the department, but no luck."

Berg wasn't surprised. He figured that Willard's killer had gotten rid of the books.

"Do you know whether Appleton or Duncan were in Cincinnati for the Chemistry Society Meeting?"

"I wondered about that myself, and I thought you'd want to know, so I checked our travel records. They both were there, which is no surprise. If for no other reason, Jerry would go to politic and Bill would go to search out a new job."

"What about the Friday that Willard was killed?"

"I didn't think to check on that," Lerner said, raising his eyebrows as he looked at Berg. "Let me see if either one was teaching that day," he said as he reached for the department's teaching schedule that he kept in the lower left drawer of his desk. "Bill Appleton taught in the morning, so I assume he was around at least for that, but I don't know for sure. Jerry Duncan doesn't teach on Fridays. He probably was here, though. I don't know of any scientific meeting he might have been to, and unless he's out of town on business, he's most always here."

Suddenly Berg thought he'd better take the chance to check further on Francois Beloit's alibi, which was now blown as far as a witness in Minneapolis was concerned.

"Let me ask you a couple of questions about Francois Beloit," he said. "Would he have had any motive to kill Ellingham, do you think?"

"Boy, I don't know," Lerner said, scratching the back of his head as he considered the question. "I'll have to think about that. Stuart said he couldn't support Francois for promotion to full professor, but I never thought Francois blamed him for that. Francois never was formally put in for the promotion. He asked me what I thought of his chances, and I told him I'd talk to Stuart. I did and reported back that the dean said his record wasn't strong enough for promotion. Francois seemed to take it okay."

"And how was his record?" Berg said.

"Borderline. He'd have made it with no problem not many years ago, but the standards keep going up. Francois's promotion will come along when he publishes some more articles."

"I know Beloit's teaching at the University of Minneapolis this semester, but have you seen him around here lately?"

"No, I haven't seen him since sometime this summer. Why the questions about Francois?"

"No particular reason, his name just came up, and I thought I'd better check it out," Berg said. He didn't want to cause Beloit and Doris Willard any more trouble if his suspicions about them had been wrong, so he thought he'd better change the subject before Lerner asked more questions he didn't want to answer.

"Do Appleton or Duncan, or Beloit for that matter, work with cyanide?"

"Like I told you about Frank Willard, I'm sure they would have no reason to. But it wouldn't be a problem for any of them to get. Hell, it wouldn't be any problem for a janitor to get it. Everyone around here has a key to the storeroom."

"Are you in the running for the deanship?" Berg asked suddenly, watching Lerner closely for a reaction.

"No, not me. I'm happy running the department," he said, showing no signs of emotion or deceit so far as Berg could tell.

"One last thing," Berg said. "Did Ellingham know about the problems you have with grant moneys?"

"No, thank heavens. He was a boy scout about that sort of thing."

"So you're lucky he's gone?" Berg asked.

"Maybe," Lerner said. "It all depends on who replaces him."

Chapter Seventeen

SIX AND A HALF MONTHS BEFORE, AS SOON AS THE KILLER FOUND OUT THAT Stuart Ellingham was going to be at the Society of Inorganic Chemist's meeting in Cincinnati, plans began taking shape. For months the hope had been to find a place where Ellingham could be dealt with out-of-town without creating suspicion. A scientific meeting had seemed the best bet.

An out-of-town location was important because the risk of being caught would be many times less if a local murder investigation could be avoided. In Cincinnati, the police could be left with little more than a body and whatever evidence one chose to leave. Plus, if everything were timed right, anybody with a story to tell would be gone before the body was discovered. The Cincinnati Police would also have less interest in the murder than the local police, who would be under pressure because Ellingham was an important man. In Cincinnati, he would be just another body.

Soon after learning about the Cincinnati meeting, the killer arranged a shopping trip to New York, where the first stop was Stern & Co. Theatrical Supply on Second Avenue.

"I need some help with wigs," the clerk heard. "A man's and a woman's."

"How close will you be to the audience?"

"Pretty close. It's a small community theater."

"Will the costumes be contemporary?"

"Yes. Current time. And I need to appear fairly conservative. The man's needs to be like a businessman's. The woman's off the shoulder just a little."

"Do you want to match your own color, or something else?"

"Brown, but dark."

"Okay, let's go over to this counter. I'll pull some things out, and once we find what you want we'll work on the size."

As is usual in a specialty store in New York, the clerk knew his business. After five minutes of showing wigs and another couple of minutes checking to see that his estimate of size was correct, the wigs were set.

"I also need some dental cotton."

The clerk went to a drawer and pulled out a package, which he put in a bag together with the wigs. After some quick figuring, he gave his customer the bill.

"That comes to a $168. Do you have a sales tax number for me?"

"No, I don't know what the theater's is. I'll just pay the tax."

"Cash or credit card?"

"Cash."

The next stop was Macy's, Thirty-fourth and Broadway. First, sunglasses. Two pairs, a man's and a woman's, each in a conservative wire frame that would have looked right for ordinary glasses. Each pair had photochromic lenses.

Then the necessary clothes. From one department came a New York Jets sweatshirt, in gray, and a blue baseball cap that said "Budweiser" across the front. In a casual wear department, the killer found blue washpants and dark blue tennis shoes in androgynous styles that seemed perfect. Purchases in another department of a dark blue, belted raincoat and a blue and green plaid scarf ended the clothes shopping. Everything was paid for in cash.

A drug store on Forty-fourth Street yielded a small package of Tampax tampons, a box of three Ramses lubricated condoms, and two pair of latex examination gloves.

The last stop was Brentano's on Fifth Avenue, to look in the latest edition of the Shooter's Bible. What the killer wanted to know was whether Ruger still made the Mark II, a .22 caliber automatic, and how much it cost. It was still for sale at a list price of about $225.

The next trip, on the Saturday after returning from New York, was 250 miles south to a city where all you needed to buy a handgun was money and the ability to sign a name and address, not necessarily your own. It was an all-day drive there and back, but by driving, airline records would be avoided. Clothes that day were a nondescript shirt, Levi's, and a pair of running shoes.

Near the outskirts of the city was a rest area with a telephone. A look in the Yellow Pages under "Guns" found what appeared to be the biggest gun dealer in town. That was the first choice because the biggest stores are usually the most impersonal.

"I want to see if you have a Ruger Mark II in stock," the clerk heard when he answered the phone.

"Yes, we have one."

"Can you give me directions? I'm coming in on the interstate from the north."

After learning how to find the store, the killer walked back to the car, sat down, and pulled a black plastic garbage bag to the front seat. From the bag came the Jets sweatshirt, male wig, and baseball cap, along with the package of dental cotton. The clothes went on and the cotton was stuffed all the way around the top gums, to puff out the upper lip and both cheeks.

Following the clerk's directions led easily to the store, but parking a block away seemed safer, since then no one in the store could see the car. Just before walking into the store, the killer put on a pair of sunglasses from Macy's. Since they had been in a shirt pocket, out of the light, the photochromic lenses were light. Not so light as to give someone an unobstructed view, but light enough not to draw attention when worn indoors.

The killer walked directly to the handgun counter. One of the biggest fears in the day's outing was having to stand around waiting for a clerk while people had a chance to pick-up on something to remember. But the store was staffed for a volume business, and a clerk came to the counter immediately.

"May I help you?" the clerk asked without seeming to pay much attention to who he was looking at.

"Yes, I'd like to see a Ruger Mark II."

The clerk went to the case next to where he was standing, opened a sliding glass door, and took out a pistol. He placed it on the counter for inspection, resting it on a rubber pad. After a quick look at the gun and its price, the sale was made.

"Will that be cash or a charge card?" the clerk asked.

"Cash. And I'd also like a box of .22 long rifle hollowpoints."

"Fine. Would you just fill out and sign this registration book for me? I'll get you rung up and wrap these for you."

The killer dealt with the registration book simply by printing in plain block letters a name and address made up to look right, and then by signing in a carefully practiced, unnatural style.

In a trash receptacle, at the first rest stop on the Interstate going north, went the sunglasses, hat, wig, and sweatshirt, along with the dental cotton, all crumpled together in the garbage bag in which they had traveled south.

One night the next week, the killer worked on the gun, following the instructions in a copycat rip-off of *The Anarchist Cookbook*. First the barrel had to be removed from the Ruger. Using a drill press, with a one thirty-second inch bit, the killer then drilled four rows of seven holes toward the rear of the barrel, on the top, bottom, and each side. This was to disperse some of the shell's power and slow the speed of the bullets below 1100 feet per second. Faster than that and the bullets would create a miniature sonic boom that would be impossible to suppress. After wiping everything clean of prints, the barrel went back on, using latex gloves.

Finishing the job of silencing the weapon was easy. Four ten-inch pieces of coat hanger wire were taped to the barrel, so that they stuck out six inches from the front of the barrel and left the newly-drilled holes uncovered. Around the barrel and over, around, and between the coat hanger wires the killer wrapped and stuffed several layers of fine steel wool. The wrapping continued until the core from a roll of paper towels could just be pushed over the steel wool that covered the barrel and the wire extension. On top of that were wrapped two layers of duct tape. A double layer of tape also went over the back of the paper towel core, to seal it to the gun, and another two layers were placed over the front of the core, to create a seal that the first shot would pierce with a .22 caliber hole.

Chapter Eighteen

IT WAS AFTER SIX WHEN BERG WALKED OUT OF JIM LERNER'S OFFICE. AS HE rounded the end of the corridor, near the sixth floor elevator, he spotted a campus telephone on the wall, and that gave him an idea. He dialed Eve's extension and then leaned his shoulder against the wall as he waited to see if she was still on campus. After three rings, she answered.

"How'd you like to go out for dinner?" Berg said.

"What's the occasion?" Eve asked, sounding both interested and curious.

"Let me surprise you. It's about a decision I have to make."

"Okay. Where are we going?"

"How about the club? I can pick you up in five minutes if you're ready."

Eve said to give her ten minutes. With extra time on his hands, Berg decided to walk to the other end of the chemistry building and take the stairs down to the fifth floor. He was curious to take another look at the stairwell where he had last seen Frank Willard. As he got to the door, he peered through its little window and looked down on the stairway on the other side of the door.

The window was made of two panes of clear glass with a smoke-colored laminate between, and, as viewed through the window, the harsh incandescent light falling on the pale green walls gave the stairway a macabre cast that caused Berg figuratively to shiver. As he looked through the window, he imagined that Willard's killer had shared that same view a week and a half before, and Berg wondered if the killer also had experienced the shiver.

The scene transmogrified as Berg pushed open the door, the macabre green of the walls now changed back to the original, uninteresting green it had been when he last saw it. Berg imagined himself the killer, walking down the stairs toward Willard, newspaper clutched in hand. Which hand? he wondered, and then in pantomime he quickly figured out how it must have been, assuming the killer walked down the right side of the stairway: Newspaper in the left hand, pointed at Willard's face, right hand free to discharge the weapon.

As Berg passed the point on the stairway where Willard had lain, he first imagined discharging the weapon, and then he himself felt transformed, because next he saw himself in Willard's place. Willard had been first startled, Berg thought. But then what? Pain, fear, resignation? He didn't know, but he could see himself falling in Willard's place, the books slipping out of his grip as his body hit the stairs.

As Berg continued down, he again saw himself as the killer. He hesitated when he reached the fifth floor landing. Did the killer go out onto the fifth floor or continue down the stairs? Berg went out the fifth floor door to see how that felt. It didn't feel good, because suddenly he felt vulnerable. The fifth floor was too close to the scene of the crime, and there were too many people who might see the killer in the corridor outside the stairwell door.

It felt better to Berg when he pushed open the door and again entered the stairwell. Strange that this place should feel more secure, but he now was confident that the killer had felt the same security and had descended in the stairwell beyond the fifth floor.

As he continued down the steps, he began to lose the feeling of rightness, and his sense of being in the killer's place began to disappear. By the time he reached the third floor landing, Berg felt there was no difference for him between staying in the stairwell and going out onto the floor. He shrugged his shoulders, walked out of the stairwell into the bright fluorescent light of the third floor corridors, and took the elevator to the first floor.

When Eve walked out of her building, Berg was standing by the passenger side of his car, waiting to greet her. He opened her door and motioned her in with a grand sweep of his arm, playing the caricature of a gentleman.

Once in the club, Berg was reminded how much it was like the officers' clubs he had belonged to in the Army. An announcement board just inside the door, decorated with someone's marking pen rendition of an Athenian temple, told them that tonight was "Greek Night . . . four savory entrees to choose from." Berg would have preferred a more dignified announcement, maybe a small, plain white card, printed in black ink. But he looked forward to the food.

Going by the bar on their way to the dining room, he noticed that a quarter of its tables were filled, mostly with people he knew to be regular customers. None of them were drunks, so far as he could tell, but over the course of a week he knew they put away a lot of booze. Maybe, he thought upon reflection, some of them were drunks, but the kind of drunks who could hide it. He tried to recall if he'd ever heard of the university police having to break up a fight in the bar, the way MP's had to do sometimes in clubs, but he didn't think he'd ever heard of that.

"Okay," Eve said as Berg held her chair as she sat. "What's the big decision you have to make?"

"How does 'Dean Berg' strike your ears?" he asked, smiling.

"It sounds good," she said cautiously. "Has the provost offered it to you?"

"No, but Mary Abbott says the search committee will support me. They'd want me to take over at the beginning of the next semester. I think the provost would go along."

"This is really sudden," Eve said, obviously concerned. "What do you think? Do you want to do it?"

"I wish I knew. There's honor to it, at least in some circles."

"Yes, but in others you'd be thought of as sleeping with the enemy, definitely without honor."

"You're right about that," Berg allowed. "But I'd consider it an honor. The only problem is, I keep thinking about the guy who was tarred and feathered and ridden out of town on a rail, and who said that if it wasn't for the honor of the thing, he'd just as soon have walked."

Eve laughed. "You really can't accept just because of the honor. Do you want to be dean? I mean, do you want to do what deans do?"

"I don't know. We need a dean who is good at fundraising. I'm not sure I'd be good at it, and I'm less sure I'd like it. And then there's the problem that I'd have everybody pulling on me in all different directions. Plus I'm not sure anyone could ever lead the bunch of prima donnas we've got on the faculty."

"Is that any different from other faculties?" Eve asked as if she knew the answer.

"No," Berg said, looking at Eve and smiling. "All professors are prima donnas. I admit it."

"How long would the appointment be for?"

"Three years, I think. But of course you can be reappointed. The thing is, it looks to me like most deans don't last longer than a couple of terms."

"Oh," Eve said. "Science deans usually stay around a long time. What's the difference?"

Berg drummed his fingers on the table. Then he said,

sounding distracted, "I'm not sure. Science deans usually don't have to do much fundraising, so it doesn't matter whether they're good at it." He was silent for a couple of minutes while Eve studied the menu. Then he said, "You know what I'm really afraid of? What would happen to me when I stopped being dean. Too many people who try it end up as failures, and by then they've convinced a lot of their old friends that they're jerks."

"What about your job with the police? You couldn't keep that, could you?"

Eve's question hit him like a brick between the eyes. He couldn't believe he hadn't thought of that. "No, I don't suppose so," he said. "I could still do something, but it couldn't be the same. I wouldn't have the time. I'd have meetings scheduled all day."

As Berg finished what he'd been saying, his right arm brushed against the revolver he carried on his hip, and a sense of loss came over him at the thought of giving up the work he loved.

Chapter Nineteen

BERG DIDN'T SLEEP WELL MONDAY NIGHT. MAYBE HE'D HAD TOO MUCH TO EAT, HE thought. And maybe the deanship was too much on his mind. The thought of giving up his current life had made his mind turn over and over as he tried to sleep, yet the thought of pushing aside the deanship offer from his old friend Mary Abbott wasn't easy to sleep on either.

As often happened when he'd a bad night trying to sleep, Berg was deep asleep in the morning when his alarm went off. He hit the snooze button twice before he could bring himself to get up, and that started him running late. Sometimes, in that circumstance, Berg would skip his morning walk, but that morning something told him he needed it.

The morning air felt cool and pleasantly damp as he stepped out his back door and fell in place behind Ginger. He was sluggish at first, but by the time his feet left the asphalt of the road that ran behind his house and hit the sandy path through his favorite field, Berg's body and mind began to clear themselves of toxins, physical and mental.

Still, he moved more slowly than usual, and Ginger ran ahead for awhile, then stopped and ran back, barking for him to hurry up.

"Give me a break," he said to the dog. "I'm doing the best I can." But Ginger paid no attention.

As Berg walked, he cast his eyes over the ground. Once in awhile, maybe every couple of weeks, he would see something that looked like it might be an arrowhead. He would always stop and look, but he had never found one. That morning, as he followed Ginger over a low hill, his eyes fell on black flint in the sandy soil of the path.

This time it was an arrowhead, and digging that arrowhead out of the sand excited him more than anything that had happened in a long time, certainly more than being told he could have a deanship. Walking along the path on the way home, he realized that he had learned something important from finding the arrowhead—that happiness comes by itself, not along with something that others place value on.

After a quick shower and breakfast, and now feeling exhilarated rather than sluggish, Berg arrived at his office and immediately picked up the telephone. "Good morning, Kate," he began when she answered, his voice upbeat. "I've come up with two possible suspects. I thought maybe we could each run some things down and then compare notes later."

"That's fine with me," Kate said, sounding not so lively that early in the morning. "What do you want me to do?"

"The names are William Appleton and Gerald Duncan. They're professors in the chemistry department. Ellingham was shot with a Ruger Mark II. Why don't you check to see if either of them has one registered." Then, after a moment's hesitation, he added, "And while you're at it, do the same for Beloit and Doris Willard, and Lerner too."

"What about Marilyn Harris?" Kate said, surprised at Berg's failure to cover all the possibilities.

"Yes, I suppose you might as well. Also, I thought you might call the local firing ranges to see if they know any of those people. Plus you could check with the city police and the NCIC computer to see if any of them has a record."

"No problem. I'll work on it this morning and call you later."

"By the way, Lerner says he hasn't seen Beloit all semester," Berg added. "For whatever that's worth."

Since his talk with Lerner, Berg had thought about his new suspects, Appleton and Duncan, and about the motives they might have had for killing Willard and Ellingham. He didn't know Duncan well or Appleton at all, but based on possible motives, he considered Appleton the likelier suspect. Berg knew that few people ever recover from being denied tenure. It often turned them into pariahs at other schools, so they were lucky if they could get another teaching job. Appleton thought he had gotten a raw deal, and Berg thought so too. That made a good motive as far as Berg was concerned.

He had decided to investigate Appleton, but as usual he didn't know how he was going to go about it. He put his feet up on his desk, leaned back in his chair, and studied the little holes in the ceiling tiles as he tried to figure out what to do. What he needed was a base of data that he could sift through to look for some place to start. He thought about calling the personnel department to see what they had in their records, but he doubted they'd have much. Perhaps Lerner's office would have at least an old curriculum vitae—the academic equivalent of a resume—and maybe even an up-to-date one, so he called Lerner's secretary.

"Check your files, will you, to see if you have a vitae for Professor Appleton, the more recent the better." Then, thinking ahead, he added, "Also for Professor Duncan, if you don't mind."

"I'm sure we have recent vitae for both of them," she said. "Professor Lerner gets them at the end of every year so he can write up a report on publications and grants. Let me pull the file."

In no more than twenty seconds, Lerner's secretary was back on the line. "Yes, I have them here from last spring."

"Would you fax them to me, please?" Berg said. "I need them right away, and I'm too lazy to come and get them."

When Berg pulled the vitae off the fax machine, he glanced at both, and then put Duncan's aside. Appleton's showed early promise. Ph.D. from a fine school, post-doctoral fellowship from another. Then slowness in getting started publishing scientific papers, followed by a flurry of activity in the year or two before his tenure review. It looked like what Berg had seen many times before—too little, too late. Perhaps, he thought, it wasn't just an unfair review that had killed Appleton's chances.

Berg opened his directory that listed the addresses and telephone numbers of university police departments around the country, along with their ranking officers. He looked up the telephone numbers of the departments at the schools where Appleton had been a graduate student and a post-doctoral fellow, and he called their chiefs.

What he wanted to know was whether Appleton had been in any trouble, and especially if there had been any murders at their schools during Appleton's time there. He also called the chair of the chemistry department where Appleton got his doctorate, and the director of the laboratory where he did his post-doc, asking them the same questions. Nothing.

Shortly after Berg finished, Kate called to say that her checks had come up negative, not only on Appleton and Duncan, but on everyone else too.

"I've looked at the university's schedule of classes," Berg said. "Appleton has a class that lets out in about a half-hour. I can't think of anything else to do, so why don't we just go see him. On the way, I can fill you in on what I've found out about Ellingham's murder and on what I learned about Appleton from Jim Lerner."

"Where are we going to talk to him?"

"Let's bring him back to the police station, if he'll come. We've got zip on him, so all we can do is try to scare something out of him."

As they waited in Kate's unmarked car for Appleton's class to let out, Berg told her what he'd learned, and they planned the interrogation. Berg was frustrated, and he felt he had to make something happen.

"Let's push him and see if anything breaks," Berg said. "I'm tired of screwing around."

"Are we going to read him his rights?" Kate asked.

"I don't know. Technically, we won't have him in custody, so the Supreme Court says we wouldn't have to. The trouble is, judges look at all that with 20/20 hindsight. If we do get anything out of him, a judge likely will believe we had him in custody whether we did or not."

"Giving him the warning will probably just help to scare him anyway," Kate said. "I think we should do it."

"Let's do it when we get him to the station then."

They stopped William Appleton outside the door of his classroom.

"William Appleton?"

"Yes."

"I'm Assistant Chief Berg of the university police," Berg said, holding up his credentials for Appleton to see, "and this is Detective Michaelman. We'd like you to come with us, please." Berg motioned for Appleton to walk toward the elevator and took a step himself, so that Appleton was carried along without having a chance to think about what was happening.

"Where are we going?" Appleton said as they approached the elevator doors.

"To the police building. Let's wait to talk until we get there."

Berg and Kate kept quiet all the way to the station, not even talking when Berg opened the rear door of the police car and motioned Appleton in. They knew that nothing would prime Appleton better than silence.

They led him into the department's interrogation room. Like most such rooms anywhere in the world, Berg imagined, it was small and windowless. It had one old wooden table and four cheap plastic chairs. On the table was a beat-up cassette recorder. The walls of the room had been painted years ago in the ubiquitous institutional-green, and they had no decoration. Berg thought that what the room really needed was some blood spattered on the walls to put suspects in the right frame of mind. He might have spattered the blood himself, except that the police used the room mostly as a lunchroom, and he didn't think they'd find bloody walls appetizing.

Kate pushed the "play" and "record" buttons on the cassette recorder and began speaking. She gave the date and time and then said, "This is Detective Catherine Michaelman. I'm in the university police interrogation room with Assistant Chief Eric Berg and Professor William Appleton." Then, turning to Appleton, she said, "It's my duty to advise you of your rights. You have the right to remain silent. Anything you say can and will be used against you in a court of law. You have the right to consult with an attorney and to have an attorney present during questioning. If you desire an attorney and cannot afford one, an attorney will be provided for you. Do you understand these rights?"

"Uh, yes."

"Are you willing to answer questions without an attorney?"

"What's this about?"

"I think you know," Kate said, staring into Appleton's eyes. "But we can't talk to you about it unless you agree to talk to us."

"Okay, okay, I'll answer questions," Appleton said, obviously nervous. "What's this about?"

"Don't insult me, Appleton. You know exactly what this is about." As planned, Kate did the interrogation. She sat in a chair across from him. Berg stood in the corner on Kate's side of the table, his arms crossed in front of him. He had taken his sport coat off and placed it, folded neatly, over one of the room's plastic chairs, so the shoulder holster he was wearing that day hung under his left arm for Appleton to see. Berg hoped for a subconscious intimidating effect.

"No, I don't," Appleton said plaintively. "I really don't."

"The two people you hated the most in this world are murdered and you tell me you don't know why you're here. Give me a break."

"I thought Frank Willard had a heart attack."

"You mean that's what you wanted us to think."

"No, I didn't have anything to do with it."

"We know all about the weapon," Kate said, as she and Berg watched Appleton's eyes for a response. "You didn't count on that did you?"

"I don't know anything about a weapon."

"Come off it," Kate said, leaning forward and putting her face a couple of feet from Appleton's. "Metal tube about this long and this big around," she added, gesturing with her hands.

Appleton again denied knowing what Kate was talking about. Berg had studied him carefully for a response, but all he saw was the same level of fear Appleton had shown all along.

"We know about the gun too. You killed Ellingham with your Ruger Mark II. Thought you were smart, didn't you? But you screwed up. Hooker, my butt. You're the one, and we've got you," Kate said, leaning back in her chair.

"No, I didn't do anything."

"How is it," Kate said suddenly, "that when I mentioned the two people you hated most in the world, you knew I was talking about Willard and Ellingham?"

Appleton shifted in his chair and began to wring his hands. "I don't know how you knew," he said, "but it's true. There isn't anybody I hated more."

"Well we do know," Kate began again. "And we also know you killed them." Then Kate said nothing else, hoping silence would work its wonders.

Appleton sat uneasily as Kate and Berg both watched him. They let a minute pass. Finally Appleton said, "I know you must have something that makes you think I killed them, but I don't know what it is."

"Screwing you on tenure gave you a good motive, don't you think?" Kate said sarcastically.

"I guess so."

"And you knew how to kill Willard with cyanide. You are a chemist, right?"

"Yes."

"And any damn fool can shoot someone with a gun, right?"

"Yes, I suppose so."

And you were in Cincinnati when Ellingham was shot and here when Willard was murdered, weren't you?"

"Yes, I admit that."

Kate locked her eyes on Appleton's. "Do you know what it will take the DA to convict you of murder?"

"No," Appleton said as he began to fidget in his chair, looking as if he would like to pace around the room.

"Means, motive, and opportunity," Kate told him. "And we've got you with all three for Willard and Ellingham. You know what that adds up to—means, motive, and opportunity?" Kate said, counting off on her fingers in front of Appleton's face.

"No."

She leaned over the table and glared at Appleton. "There's capital punishment in this state. The district attorney will ask for the death penalty, and you'll get it. That's what it means."

Seeing the look on Appleton's face, Berg took hold of Kate's arms and pulled her back. "Detective Michaelman, wait for me outside."

"I'm not through with him," she said, making it clear that she didn't like Berg's butting in.

"I'm not taking a vote here, detective," Berg said, measuring his words carefully. "I told you to wait outside."

Showing by her exprcssion that she was miffed, Kate shoved herself out of her chair and left the room.

Berg sat down next to Appleton. "She really doesn't understand the situation, Bill," Berg began. "Besides being with the police, I'm a professor. I know what Ellingham and Willard did to you. Detective Michaelman wants to turn these deaths into something we both know they aren't. You need to come clean with me. I promise that if you do—and I'm putting this right on the tape—if you do, I'll do everything I can for you with the district attorney."

"But I didn't do anything."

"No one's ever going to believe that. We've got too much evidence and the Cincinnati Police have too much evidence. You can get executed for either murder, you know. They've got two separate trials to do it in." Berg didn't know whether they had capital punishment in Ohio or not, and probably Appleton didn't either, because he didn't call Berg's bluff.

Appleton put his head in his hands and began to rub his temples.

"If you'll talk to me," Berg continued, "I'll do everything I can for you."

"I'll talk to you. There just isn't anything I can say."

"I'm going to let Detective Michaelman come back in here. I'll keep her off you if you cooperate. We'll just take it a step at a time."

Berg went to the door and let Kate back in. They both sat down this time, Kate across from Appleton and Berg between them, his gun on Kate's side of the table, following procedure.

"Okay," Berg began. "Let's make this easy. You hated Ellingham and Willard because they ruined your career. That's right, isn't it?"

"They ruined my life."

"I agree. And you hated them."

"Yes, I've already said I hated them."

"And you wanted them dead? Don't try to tell me you didn't want them dead."

"Yes, I wanted them dead," Appleton admitted.

"As anybody would. So you decided to go to Cincinnati, where you knew Ellingham would be?"

"No, I swear I didn't know."

Kate leaned forward before Appleton could finish and said loudly, "Crap! I'm not going to sit here and listen to your drivel. You knew damn well Ellingham would be at the chemistry meeting. It was announced right in the brochure."

Appleton moved back in his chair as if trying to get away from Kate. And he looked at Berg seeming to ask for his help. Then he admitted, "Yes, all right, I knew he'd be there."

"Let me just take this idiot down to the county jail and book him," Kate said angrily.

Appleton looked to Berg like a little boy who had been caught lying about sneaking a cookie before dinner. "Let's give him a little more chance," Berg told her. "Bill, we just caught you lying, and it won't work. We know too much. You've got to tell us the truth the first time through. I can't help you if you won't do that."

"Okay," Appleton said, sheepishly.

"So you saw Ellingham in Cincinnati," Berg said.

"Yes, I saw him there."

"And Friday night you went to his room."

"No, no" Appleton said loudly. "I never went to his room."

"Bill," Berg said soothingly, "don't let's go down that road again."

"I swear it's the truth. I never went to his room."

"Don't try to tell us you didn't want to kill him. You did, didn't you?"

"No," Appleton said, but as he said it his eyes shifted away from Berg's, and the tone of his voice showed no conviction. Berg decided to let Appleton stew in his lie, so he just sat looking at him, saying nothing.

Soon Appleton spoke, appearing to know he'd been caught lying again. "Okay, I admit I wanted to kill Ellingham."

"Tell us about it." Berg said.

"Well, I thought about it. I thought about buying a gun and killing him, but I didn't do it."

"And Willard, you thought about killing him too, didn't you?"

"Yes, I admit that too," Appleton said, evidently having learned that getting away with lying to the police wasn't easy.

"Let's talk about Willard. As Detective Michaelman said, we know you killed Willard, we know all about the weapon. If you won't tell us the truth, I'm going to have to let Detective Michaelman handle this the way she wants to. It's her case."

"I don't know what you're talking about," Appleton said, as if pleading with Berg to believe him. "I swear I thought he died of a heart attack. I was glad he died, and I was glad when Ellingham got killed, but I didn't have anything to do with any of it."

"That's mighty convenient, isn't it?" Kate said. "You're the one person who hated them both, had reason to kill them both, thought about killing them both, and other people just happened to kill them for you. If you think a jury'll believe that, you're crazy."

"Look," Berg said, "I can see that you don't want to get involved in Ellingham's murder. To tell you the truth, that's smart. One killing a good lawyer can do something with, but even Alan Dershowitz probably couldn't do much with two. Plus, to be honest with you, we really don't much care whether the Cincinnati Police solve Ellingham's murder. Come clean on Willard, and we won't ask you any more questions about Ellingham. As far as we're concerned, that will be it. Plus my offer still holds. I'll do all I can for you with the DA."

As Appleton started to respond, Kate again leaned forward and looked into his eyes, "You give us any more bullshit and, I swear, I'm taking you right to jail."

Appleton looked down at the table and said, "I didn't do it. I didn't kill either one of them."

Berg and Kate kept still. After only ten seconds, Appleton didn't seem to be able to stand the silence any longer. "I would have killed them if I could have, but I didn't have the guts. The bastards ruined my life, and I was still afraid to kill them." Appleton sounded as if he were ashamed. He put his head down and said again, "I didn't have the guts to kill them."

After waiting a full minute to see if more was coming, Berg got up and said, "Detective Michaelman, let's step out for a minute."

They went down the hall to Kate's office. When Kate closed the door, Berg said, "What do you think?"

"I don't think there's anything there to get. I saw lots of fear, but I never saw the right responses, especially when we hit him with the evidence."

"That's what I think. I don't believe he's a good enough actor to put on the performance he did. Now you, Kate, that's another question," Berg said, winking.

"I thought we made a pretty good team."

"Yeah, but I had the easy part," Berg said. "Why don't we keep you on deck in case we need to talk to him again. That way you can pick up where you left off. I can drive him back and comfort him a little."

"You do make a good nice guy," Kate said, smiling as she handed him the keys to the car.

When he walked back into the interrogation room, Appleton looked up with a mixture of fear and anticipation. When Berg said, "We've decided to let you go," Appleton let out a sigh of relief and smiled weakly.

As they were moving toward the police car, Berg worked over in his mind the irony—here was a guy who was sad an hour ago because he'd lost his job, and now he's happy because he isn't going to the electric chair.

See what good I do in the world, Berg thought, trying to make himself happy by being funny. But it didn't work because he wasn't comfortable with the job he and Kate had done on Appleton. He wondered if they hadn't beaten up on Appleton just because he was a weak and easy target and they were frustrated.

Berg felt sorry enough—either sorry for Appleton or sorry about how he and Kate had treated him—that on the way back to the chemistry building he did something totally against police doctrine.

"Look, Bill," he said. "If you've been telling the truth, don't worry about this afternoon. Nothing's going to happen to you."

Chapter Twenty

ELLINGHAM'S KILLER HAD MADE A DECISION TO TRY FOR HIM AT THE HILTON IN Cincinnati. The hotel was where the chemistry meeting was to be, and Ellingham was sure to stay there. The choice that had to be made was, drive or fly? It was a long trip by car, but driving would avoid the slim chance that the airline would X-ray checked baggage, so driving it was. The only thing to do before Friday night was learn Ellingham's room number.

Ellingham should arrive sometime Friday, since he was to receive his award that evening. To find out for sure, the killer picked the airline and flight that seemed most likely, and, pretending to be calling for Ellingham, told the agent that Ellingham wanted to confirm his reservation. The agent said he was confirmed on flight sixty-one.

After checking the arrival time of Ellingham's plane on Friday morning, and walking to the rank of cabs waiting outside the hotel to ask about driving time from the airport, it was easy to learn when to expect him.

The lobby was a large place swirling with people, so there was no problem waiting there unnoticed. At the expected time, Ellingham stepped out of a taxi and walked to the check-in desk. As the clerk seemed about to give him his key, the killer walked toward the reception desk, trying to hear the clerk tell Ellingham his room number. The timing was off, and that failed. The next chance was when a bellman met Ellingham and asked for his room number. That didn't work either, so only the least favored option was left, following Ellingham to his room.

Entering the elevator with Ellingham and the bellman, the killer was able to get a place just inside the doors, on the front next to the elevator buttons, not noticeable unless Ellingham was paying attention. He wasn't, but spent the ride talking to the bellman. When the elevator stopped, Ellingham and the bellman stepped off, and the killer followed them into the corridor, lagging as far behind as possible without seeming strange.

As they went farther and farther down the corridor, it looked like Ellingham might have one of the last rooms. It would be best simply to walk near the room and get the number without attracting attention, but that would be hard to do if there was nowhere to walk except to the fire stairs. But the bellman opened a door several rooms from the end, and they were inside quickly.

By ten o'clock that night, everything was ready. Anytime between then and eleven or so would be ideal—not many people walking around, but enough so that no one person would stick out. A call to Ellingham's room at ten got no answer. Fifteen minutes later, the same.

The Labcoat

At ten thirty, Ellingham picked up the phone and said hello. The killer said nothing, but listened intently. What was important was to hear if anyone was in the background, and all seemed quiet.

Wearing a tan windbreaker over a sportshirt, plus the man's brown wig, blue washpants, and blue tennis shoes bought in New York, the killer walked into the hallway, carrying the Ruger under the windbreaker and a blue sports bag in hand.

On the way to Ellingham's room, no familiar face appeared, and there was no one in the hallway outside Ellingham's room. After a quiet rap, the door opened a few seconds later. The Ruger now came out from under the windbreaker and was pushed into Ellingham's stomach, backing Ellingham into his room.

"What's this?" Ellingham began, but the killer quieted him by hissing "shush" and thrusting the gun forward. The combination of gesture and sound had the desired effect, and Ellingham remained quiet.

The killer dropped the sports bag, walked to the television, and pushed the "power" button with an elbow, so as to leave no prints. When it came on, the killer calmly shot Ellingham once through the forehead and watched him fall.

Examination gloves were taken from a jacket pocket and pulled on. This allowed the cold water to be turned full on in the bathtub without leaving prints, and then the killer returned to where Ellingham lay and fired three shots into Ellingham's groin and then one through an eye, to make sure he'd have enough brain damage to die for sure and quickly. These shots were noisier than the first because the duct tape across the front of the gun no longer formed a seal, and because some of the steel wool used to quiet the sound had been blown out. But the sound of the gun was still highly suppressed, and there was little danger that it would be heard above the noise of the television and the bathtub.

The killer went to the sports bag, unzipped it, and dropped in the Ruger. Out of the bag came a condom and a piece of a tampon wrapper about an inch long. After walking back into the bathroom and turning off the water, the tampon wrapper was dropped by the wastebasket. On the way out of the bathroom, two facial tissues were pulled from the dispenser next to the mirror.

The killer walked to the nightstand and laid down one tissue, on which was placed the condom after it was freed from its foil wrapper. The wrapper went into the sports bag so that prints were not left, nor was suspicion created by not leaving any. The five spent shell casings also went into the sports bag.

Stopping for a few seconds to listen, and hearing nothing except the television, the killer pulled from the sports bag the dark brown woman's wig. After carefully checking the adjustment in the mirror by the door, next came dental cotton over the killer's upper gum, and the woman's glasses with photochromic lenses.

The final new clothes were the blue and green scarf and the blue raincoat. The last thing to come from the sports bag was a paper shopping bag with plastic handles, into which the sports bag was shoved. The final steps in the room were again to push the television's "power" button and then pull off the examination gloves and drop them in the shopping bag.

When looking out the peephole showed that no one was near the room, the doorknob, wrapped with a facial tissue, was turned and the door opened a crack, so any noises could be heard from farther down the hallway. All was quiet. The killer took a last look around to see that nothing had been missed, and then, with the tissue in hand, put the Do Not Disturb sign on the outside doorknob. Still hearing and seeing no one, the killer stepped into the hallway, pulled the door shut, and walked though the door to the fire stairs.

Inside the door, the killer listened for a second to see if anyone else was in the stairwell and, hearing no one, began walking down the steps, all the way to the first floor.

Upon reaching the first floor, the shopping bag went on the floor and the sports bag was pulled out. Into that went everything put on in Ellingham's room, along with the shopping bag, and back on went the man's wig. Because it had been practiced often, this all took less than ten seconds.

The killer listened at the door to see if anyone was outside. Hearing nothing, and again using the tissue over the doorknob, the killer walked confidently out into the first floor of the hotel, casually putting the tissue in a windbreaker pocket. No one had been near the door, and no one paid any attention on the walk to the elevator.

The killer went to bed, slept soundly, and was checked out by nine the next morning.

Chapter Twenty-One

BACK IN HIS OFFICE AFTER THE INTERROGATION OF WILLIAM APPLETON, BERG decided to turn to Jerry Duncan as a suspect, and to ask Kate to interview Marilyn Harris. That, he thought, had been put off too long. He called Kate.

"I'd like to make some calls about Duncan. How about your talking to Marilyn Harris? I'm done interviewing women, at least by myself. I haven't figured out anything yet from talking to them."

"Anything special you want me to push?" Kate asked.

"All I can think of are the books she got lost for us. What she told me about the books never made any sense to me. Also, about her relationship with Willard and the story of his ruined manuscript."

"And her relationship with Duncan, if she has one," Kate added.

"Yes, that too. Let's talk later."

The first thing Berg did was call the university police where Duncan had been a post-doctoral fellow. That turned up nothing. Neither did a call to the director of the laboratory where Duncan had done the fellowship. It was different, though, when Berg talked to the chief of the university police where Duncan had been a graduate student. Even though it was almost fifteen years in the past, the chief remembered a murder that happened when Duncan was a student there. The chief promised to pull the file and call Berg back. A few minutes later, he did.

"This is better for you than I remembered, or worse, depending on your point of view," the chief began. "Gerald Duncan's name shows up in the report. Or I should say, reports. What I've got here is our report plus a copy of the state police report. They had jurisdiction."

Berg could feel his excitement building when he heard that Duncan had been somehow involved in the case. There was no doubt what his point of view was. He wanted a good suspect, and so far he hadn't been able to develop much solid on anyone else.

"Let me hear what you've got," he said.

The chief cleared his throat and began to speak, picking facts out of his department's report. "One night at about half past ten someone found a professor's body in the parking lot near where he worked. The body was next to his car. He'd been shot once in the back of the head with a .22. He was a chemistry professor named Henry Enderman. We never solved the case."

"How did Jerry Duncan come in?"

"Turned out Enderman had been on Duncan's dissertation committee."

"Was Duncan a suspect?" Berg asked, his hopes rising.

"Not really. We interviewed him and the state police did too. One of the other committee members said Enderman had been giving Duncan problems about the draft of his dissertation, but it evidently didn't amount to much. The other members didn't agree with Enderman. They also told us that Enderman typically gave graduate students a hard time, but that he always came around in the end. The other committee members said they were sure Duncan knew everything would be fine with his dissertation. All he would have needed was their votes anyway, so Enderman wouldn't have mattered in the end."

"But you interviewed him."

"Yes, nothing interesting turned up, though. He never seemed like he had anything to hide. He said he was working in the library, which is a couple of buildings over from where the body was found. He gave us the names of some people who were sitting near him. They said he was at the library, although no one could account for him all the time. But then they couldn't account for each other's time for the whole evening either, what with trips to the snack bar, phone calls, and general screwing around."

"Do you mind giving me the names of the other people on the committee? I need to get a better picture of Duncan, and I'd like to talk to them."

"No problem. Daniel Wright and Helen Milligan are the names I have here. Professor Wright evidently was his main advisor. Would you like me to get their phone numbers for you?"

"That would be great."

Berg was able to get Wright's number, but after checking in the university telephone book and then a faculty register, the chief was only able to tell Berg that Helen Milligan had been given emeritus status five years before. No address was listed.

"Okay, that's fine. I won't worry about Milligan. What else did you have on the murder?"

"The state police thought it was a hired killing. It had all the earmarks of it. Use of a .22. Enderman evidently was kneeling when he was shot. The placement of the wound was perfect, right at the base of his skull."

"Who did they think paid for the killing?"

"Their best suspect was Enderman's wife. I agreed too. There had been marital problems. Real nasty ones, as I remember. Also, the wife got married not long after her husband died. I'm sure she knew it would seem suspicious, but she knew by then that no one had any evidence on her."

"I don't suppose the weapon ever turned up?"

"No, fat chance," the chief said. "The state police lab was able to do good analysis on the bullet, but no one ever found a gun to match it to."

"One of my murders was with a .22. Do you have ballistics data in your report? Does it say what kind of .22 it was?"

"The lab sent us a photograph of the bullet, but nothing here says anything about what kind of gun, just the caliber."

Berg had an idea. "If I get you a number, would you fax that picture to the Cincinnati police? I want to see if we can get a match."

"Absolutely."

"I'll call you, or someone will, in a few minutes."

Berg felt elated. Finally it looked like something definite might break his whole case. He got through to Bill Clampton, his contact at the Cincinnati police detective bureau, who promised to walk the faxed picture through ballistics.

Berg arranged the fax and then, without putting down the telephone, punched in the number of Duncan's dissertation adviser.

"Dr. Wright's lab," a young female voice said.

Berg asked for Wright and then waited, listening over the phone to rock music and laughter coming from the lab. Two minutes later, Wright picked up the phone, and the music stopped, Berg assumed because the telephone was in Wright's office and he had shut his door.

"I'd like to ask about a former student of yours, Gerald Duncan," Berg began.

"Okay," Wright said, drawing the word out. It sounded to Berg as if Wright wasn't really sure he wanted to talk about Duncan. "Can you tell me first what this is about?"

Ordinarily Berg didn't want someone to know why he was asking questions, but this time he thought it was just as well. "Sure," he replied. "He's a suspect in a murder case, or rather in two of them."

"Oh my."

"I'm calling to ask you about a murder on your campus when Duncan was a graduate student. The murder of Henry Enderman."

"I remember it well. We haven't had a murder here before or since."

"Did anyone think Duncan killed Henry Enderman?" Berg asked.

"I don't really know. Lots of people were talking about all kinds of crazy theories. I think Jerry's name came up."

"Do you know why?"

"Well," Wright said, hesitating, "some people don't understand Jerry. He comes across stone cold a lot of the time. And then, too, people knew that Henry had been giving Jerry trouble about his dissertation, threatening not to approve it."

"Was that going to be a problem or not?"

"No, it wasn't. The rest of the committee thought Jerry's dissertation was fine. It was excellent in fact. We would have approved it, and that would have been that."

"Did Jerry know that?"

"I asked myself that after Henry was killed. I never told Jerry in so many words that his dissertation would have been approved irrespective of what Henry thought, but it had to have been clear to him. I was particularly strong in my praise of his work, and so was the other committee member. Jerry could do simple arithmetic and see that two to one would get his dissertation approved in the worst case. He's shown I was right too—about his work, I mean. He's become a very important man in the field."

"I don't understand the 'stone cold' part of what you've told me. I've heard that he's a good politician. He's in the running for a deanship, and that takes someone who can deal with people."

"Jerry can deal with people on a certain level. Let me put it this way—he's the kind of guy who will be careful to remember your wife's name and to ask about her, but he doesn't come across as caring much what you tell him back."

"Doesn't sound like a very nice guy," Berg allowed.

"You could say that, but I know him pretty well. There isn't a mean bone in his body. I'd say he's preoccupied. He puts everything he has into his career."

"So what if Enderman really had been in the way of his career, or if Duncan merely felt he was in the way? Would you have considered him a good suspect then?" Berg asked.

"Well, I don't know," Wright responded, again drawing out his words. "Who knows what a person will do when his back is against the wall?"

When his conversation with Wright was over, Berg began pacing his office. This time it was partly due to his excitement over what he had learned about Duncan, but also from anticipation of what the Cincinnati police ballistics lab could come up with on the bullets that had killed Enderman and Ellingham.

He sat down and picked up the latest issue of a scholarly journal on theology, which usually interested him. Or at least the table of contents did, for that gave him a quick idea of whether anyone else had beat him out by publishing something close to what he was working on. Like all professors, one of Berg's greatest fears was finding that an article he had put massive effort into was not publishable. He took his usual interest in the table of contents, but then couldn't get interested in reading any of the articles. Mostly he walked around the room or just sat and waited.

A call from Kate ended his wait. She had a story to tell about Marilyn Harris.

"The woman's a real bitch," Kate said. "She didn't even try to be helpful—in fact, she didn't even try to seem like she was trying to be helpful."

"What about the books?"

"She just blew me off about those. Said nobody wanted Willard's textbooks, so she couldn't see what the fuss was about. Denied knowing anything about them and still swears she put them in the bookcase outside his office."

"And her relationship with Willard?"

"There she was a little more forthcoming, though I don't think she knew it. It's clear she hated him, especially for trying to get her fired. But it was weird. When I asked her about the destroyed manuscript chapters, I got the same hint of a Cheshire cat grin that Lerner did. So far as what she said, though, that was another story. She says she doesn't know how the chapters got destroyed, except that computers were new to her."

"And what about her and Duncan?"

"Just that they went to a couple of department parties together and had dinner a few times. Wouldn't admit that she cared about whether they saw each other again or not."

"Did you believe her?"

"No."

"Where does the 'bitch' part come in?"

"Just her attitude. Like we get from teenagers we throw off campus because we think they are up to something—'You've got nothing on me so get out of my face.' That kind of thing."

"Maybe I'll have to go back to interviewing women, Kate. She was perfectly sweet to me."

"Well you can have her."

"On a happier note," Berg said, hoping to lift Kate's mood. "I've got something going on Duncan. One of his Ph.D. advisors got murdered fifteen years ago, and with a .22 to boot. The Cincinnati Police are comparing ballistics now, and I need to get off the line so they can reach me."

He didn't have long to wait. Within a half-hour, Bill Clampton called from Cincinnati.

"The lab says there's no match on the bullets. Definitely different guns."

Berg was deflated, literally. He let out a breath and his shoulders stumped from the letdown he felt. "It was too good to hope for," he said.

Clampton picked up on Berg's disappointment. "It gets better, though," he added. "They also say that the gun used fifteen years ago was a Ruger Mark II. No doubt about it. Maybe we've got the same guy, but he's too smart to keep a murder weapon around for fifteen years."

"We may well have," Berg said, now disappointed in himself for underrating Duncan. He knew he shouldn't have expected someone as smart as Duncan to get caught with a murder weapon.

Chapter Twenty-Two

IT HAD BEEN A VERY LONG TUESDAY MORNING, ESPECIALLY SINCE BERG DIDN'T think of a morning as over until lunch. After talking to Bill Clampton, it was almost two o'clock, and Berg hadn't had time for lunch.

He picked up the telephone again almost as soon as he put it down and dialed Kate's number. "Kate," he said when he heard her voice, "had lunch?"

"No, I've been catching up on paperwork I'm behind on because of you."

"Well, I was going to suggest that you buy me lunch, but maybe I should buy it for you. Let's go to the club. I want to fill you in on what I've found out about Jerry Duncan."

"That's the best offer I've had today," she said.

Berg drove to the police building to pick up Kate. On the way he began to feel nervous, which seemed strange to him. Why he should be nervous about going to lunch, he didn't know. He finally decided that what he was feeling was anticipation. It was the feeling he used to get in college on the way to pick up a date. He hadn't felt that way in a long time. The feeling was good, but uncomfortable.

Berg's sense of anticipation continued as they were shown to a table for two in the corner of the smallest downstairs room at the faculty club. As they talked, he caught himself comparing Kate to Janet Miller, and he found that she compared very favorably.

After ordering lunch, he began telling Kate what he had found out about Jerry Duncan. By the time their entrees came, she knew everything Berg did about Duncan and the murder earlier of Henry Enderman.

"We'd better talk to Duncan, don't you think?" Berg asked.

"I don't have any better idea. There's nothing else we can do at this point."

Berg had an idea, but he wasn't sure he wanted to suggest it. The idea could be touchy with Kate. Finally he went ahead. "There's one thing," he began. "I've been thinking about Beloit's five thousand dollars. I doubt he'll know what kind of sources we have, and if he does want to complain about us, I don't know who he'd complain to who'd listen. So I think we ought to chance confronting him."

"I guess as long as you keep Upshaw out of it," Kate said uncertainly. I've made promises to him."

"I bet you have," Berg said, leering and smiling at the same time.

"Not those kind of promises, you jerk," Kate said as she laughed. "So what do you want to do now?"

Berg leered again.

"About Beloit and Duncan," Kate said. This time she smiled.

"After lunch, let's call Beloit's lab in Minneapolis. We can do it from one of the phones in the member's lounge. Even if we just leave a message that we've called, that ought to keep some pressure up. Then let's go see Duncan."

"Sounds like a plan."

After lunch, Berg and Kate's telephone call found Beloit in his lab. Berg kept the top of the phone away from his ear and Kate sat close enough to hear what Beloit said, close enough that her body and Berg's gently touched.

"Francois," Berg began. "How was the rest of your stay in Chicago?"

"You can guess. You spoiled what would have been a great weekend. Besides, Doris needed me."

"Yes, I bet. But that's not why I called. Why did you take five thousand dollars in cash out of your bank account just before Willard was killed?"

Berg wished he could study Beloit's expressions and body actions, but he had to settle for what he could hear over the phone. As he listened, he first heard silence, then anger. Whether real or not, Berg couldn't tell.

"How did you get that information?"

"We have our ways, as you already know from my finding you in Chicago."

"Well, you can stuff your ways. I'm not putting up with any more of this."

"So you say. But you may be putting up with this until they strap you into 'old sparky.'" Then after a pause to let the thought sink in, Berg continued. "So what about the five thousand?"

"It's none of your business, and I'm not saying."

"Why's that, if you've got nothing to hide?"

"Because I don't like being hassled and you've become a real son of a bitch."

"I'm sorry if you don't like the way murder investigations are conducted," Berg said. "But you're going to have to answer my questions, now or later."

"Screw you," Beloit said. Then he hung up.

"So?" Berg said.

"Don't know. Obviously he moves up as a suspect. But we can't do any more on that now."

"Regrettably," he said with a sigh, "but someday I'm going to knock him on his ass." Berg was getting tired of going nowhere fast and didn't appreciate being hung up on. Then he added resignedly, "Let's go talk to Duncan and see if we can move him up or down the list."

Kate too was getting exasperated. "Fine with me," she said, without much conviction.

"How do you want to do it? At the station again?"

"I think we need to decide what we want to accomplish," Kate said thoughtfully. "One thing I don't want to do is foul up anything." From her tone, Berg could tell that she wasn't impressed by his performance with Beloit.

"From what I know about Duncan, he's not the scared rabbit type."

"Then we shouldn't give him the rubber hose treatment until we've got some hard evidence," Kate said. "Especially considering his status around here," she added, her voice seeming to show a grudging acknowledgment of the university's hierarchy. "Anyway, if we handled him like we did Appleton and it didn't work, we'd have had our one shot. You can never get the same effect the second time."

"Okay, let's just try to take the measure of him."

"And maybe see what we can get out of him while letting him think he's got us snowed." Kate paused, thinking. "Unless you want me to do otherwise, I think you should interview him while I see what I can pick up from his responses. It'll be easier that way if you want me to play the bad guy with him later."

"That's fine with me. From what Lerner told me, Duncan is usually in his lab working. Let's just drop in and see if we can find him there."

A few minutes later, they walked into Duncan's laboratory and found his office, which was tucked inside his lab the way Willard's was. Berg stuck his head in the doorway.

"Jerry?" Berg began.

The Labcoat

"Oh, hi Eric," Duncan said, looking up from his desk. He was five foot eight and slim. Short hair, light brown, and wearing a white labcoat over a sportshirt and slacks.

"Just wanted to talk to you a bit. This is Catherine Michaelman from the university police. We're working on Willard's death, and we'd like to speak with you if you can give us a few minutes."

"That's fine. I can use the break. By the way, would you like some coffee? We keep a coffeemaker in the lab. The graduate students are here half the night and they need it."

"Yes, please," Berg responded, knowing that cups in hand would buy them time in Duncan's office if they wanted it, at least until the cups were empty.

"I'll have some too, thanks," Kate said.

When they were settled in with the coffee, Berg started.

"We're trying to get a picture of where people were the day Frank Willard died. Do you remember where you were?"

"From what I've heard about when Frank died, I must have left a few minutes before it happened. I'd been working in my office most of the day. I left at about half past two."

"May I ask where you went?"

"I went home to goof off. I come in pretty early, and usually I work at night, but I split it up. I often go home for a couple of hours during the day."

"Is there anyone who would know when you arrived home that day?"

"I doubt it. I live alone. There's no reason anyone would have seen me or paid any attention if they had. Do I assume you think Frank was murdered? That's what the rumors are around here."

"Frankly, we don't know. Do you know anyone who would have wanted to kill him?"

"No, absolutely not. Frank was a very nice guy. I don't know why anyone would want to kill him."

"We know he was on some tenure committees—chaired at least one—and that one of the people he helped turn down is very bitter. Don't you think someone like that might have wanted him dead?"

"I just don't see that. I know who you're talking about. He wouldn't kill anybody."

If Duncan was the killer, Berg was impressed. Duncan obviously knew he was talking about Appleton and probably knew Appleton well enough to realize that the police wouldn't believe he was the killer once they'd investigated. So it would be smart for Duncan not to take the bait Berg offered of throwing suspicion on someone else. Berg decided to switch gears.

"We think Ellingham's murder was tied in."

Berg saw Duncan's eyes narrow a bit, and he seemed to pull back a little. "Oh, really?" he said.

"Yes, do you know anyone who might have had a motive for killing both of them?"

"No, sure don't."

"You were in Cincinnati when he was killed?"

Berg thought he detected some new reaction, but he wasn't sure, and didn't know what to make of it anyway. As Berg was thinking about this, Duncan simply said "Yes."

"Did you see him there?"

"Not so far as I know."

Berg decided to try a little trick. "What if I told you someone has said she saw you talking to him the night he was killed."

Duncan was unperturbed. "I'd say she was mistaken."

Again Berg was impressed at how cool Duncan was, assuming he had anything to hide. Berg wondered how the killer had gotten the pistol to Cincinnati, and he decided to see what Duncan had to say about that.

"How did you travel to Cincinnati?"

"I drove."

"Isn't that unusual? It must have been about an all day drive."

"It was. I didn't know for sure I was going until just before the meeting began, and I hadn't bought an airline ticket. They're too expensive if you don't buy them ahead of time."

Berg knew from experience that you usually couldn't get a room at the headquarters hotel by the time a meeting is about to begin, and he bet Duncan had made reservations in advance.

"Where did you stay?"

"At the Hilton."

"And you were able to get reservations at the last minute?" Berg said, trying to show surprise rather than incredulity.

"I knew that I might be going, so I made the reservations a long time before. It didn't cost anything."

Berg watched Duncan's eyes carefully.

"Have you ever owned a Ruger Mark II?"

"No."

Berg saw some response, but he didn't read it as surprise. Maybe Duncan knew enough about ballistics to figure the police could tell what kind of gun had been used.

"How is it you know what a Ruger Mark II is?"

Now Berg saw confusion. Was Duncan trying to decide how big a lie he should tell, especially since he'd told Berg at the faculty club that he didn't know anything about guns?

"I don't. I just know I've never owned anything called a Ruger Mark II."

"Have you ever owned a .22?"

"No."

Berg noted that Duncan's confidence was back, but he wondered if Duncan thought he'd blown it on the Ruger. Berg thought he had.

"What can you tell us about Henry Enderman's murder?"

There! Berg saw Duncan flinch. You didn't expect that, did you? Berg thought.

"I can't really tell you anything about it. It happened a long time ago. Why are you asking me about that?"

"We're just trying to run down all the possible angles. Someone brought up the fact that Enderman had been murdered when you were a graduate student. Do you know how he was murdered?"

"He was shot."

"With what kind of gun? Can you help us out there?"

Berg wondered whether Duncan would realize that an innocent man who'd never even owned a .22 probably wouldn't remember what gun had been used in a crime fifteen years before. How many people, Berg asked himself, remember the caliber of the gun that killed John Kennedy?

"I think it was a .22."

"Do you know what a .22 is, what the number refers to exactly?"

"No. The size of the gun somehow."

"How do you think it is you remember that number from fifteen years ago?"

"I don't know, I just do."

Berg thought it was time to back off.

"I was just curious," he said "I often think about how funny the mind is. I can remember what color dress my fifth-grade teacher wore on the first day of school, but I get in trouble with my wife for complimenting her on a 'new' dress that she's had for years. Weird, isn't it?"

"You can say that again," Duncan said, seeming relieved.

"I really appreciate your time, and I'm sorry to bother you with questions you may find offensive. We're just trying to check people off the list. Don't take offense."

"Oh, I haven't. I hope you find who you're looking for, if Frank was murdered."

When they were back in Berg's car, he asked Kate what she thought.

"He moves to the top of the list," she said.

"Agreed."

Chapter Twenty-Three

BERG DROPPED KATE OFF AT HER OFFICE AFTER THEIR INTERVIEW WITH DUNCAN, then started home. It was early to quit for the day, especially since he hadn't done a bit of divinity school work, but he was beat. Being tired relaxed him, and in that state he enjoyed the sensations of driving his Corvette, daydreaming as the low rumble of the car's dual exhausts worked a hypnotic effect, relaxing him further.

As he drove along, he thought of the black flint arrowhead he had found in the sand that morning and he remembered how happy it had made him. He also thought of his distress of the night before, as he had contemplated giving up his current life for a deanship. He decided once and for all that the deanship was not for him.

After giving Eve a quick kiss, Berg headed for his den—the only room in the house where she allowed him free reign. He'd had bookcases built-in over walnut paneling, covering all the available wall space that wasn't taken up by a couch and what people were now calling an "entertainment center," but what Berg called a television and stereo. The bookcases were filled, floor to ceiling, with Berg's eclectic collection of books, plus assorted memorabilia going back to his Army days. Slouched down in his easy chair with his legs stretched over an ottoman, he napped until dinnertime, the day's newspaper lying mostly unread on his lap. By the time Eve woke him, he had made up for the sleep he lost the night before.

Berg and his wife had an understanding about dinners at home. Eve cooked when she felt like it. Otherwise they ate from the supermarket's frozen food cases. That night she cooked, and when she cooked they lingered longer than when they ate out of the freezer. As they finished dinner, she mentioned something that she thought concerned her more than her husband, since she worked in the College of Science. "I heard," she said, "that our outside candidate to replace Stuart Ellingham doesn't know if she'll stay in the search."

"Oh," Berg said, just to make a polite response.

"A real tragedy. Her eight-year-old daughter was badly burned in a fire, and most of their house was destroyed. She just doesn't know if she'll have the time or energy to continue interviews."

Berg felt the familiar tightening in his stomach, this time partly because hearing about a burned girl brought back unhappy thoughts of napalm and Vietnam and partly because his instincts told him the fire was tied to the Willard case. "What happened?" he asked, showing a mixture of feelings that Eve seemed to find confusing.

Furrowing her brow as she put down her dessert fork, she replied, "Somebody firebombed her house last Saturday night."

Berg sat up and blinked his eyes. "Do you know any more about it?" he asked.

"Not really. She's Jewish, and that had something to do with it. That's all I heard."

Eve told him that it happened in a college town about fifty miles away. Berg thought it an unlikely place for vicious anti-Semitic violence, but who could tell.

"What's her name?"

"Janovitz. Harriet Janovitz."

Berg got up from the table, dropping his napkin on his chair. He called the police department in the Janovitz's town and got connected to the duty detective, convinced now more than ever that Duncan was most likely their killer.

"What can I do for you, Chief?" the detective asked.

"I'm interested in a firebombing you had last Saturday. The Janovitz house."

"You didn't have to give me the name. We don't have much of that kind of thing around here. It happened when I was on call."

"Let me ask you first off, do you think it was anti-Semitic?"

"Some maybe. There's evidence that the Janovitz's being Jewish had something to do with it, but I'm pretty sure it was mostly personal."

From what the detective had said, Berg began to see the now familiar pattern emerging. "Have you had anything else like this?" Berg asked. "Anti-Semitic I mean."

"Closest thing we had was some morons painting swastikas on the Jewish community center a couple of years ago—thought it was a funny prank until the judge made them clean the building with toothbrushes and turpentine. But we checked on them. They're off at college."

"So what was the evidence that the Janovitz's being Jewish had something to do with the crime?" Berg said, realizing too late that his tone was condescending, because he doubted the evidence before he had even heard it.

The detective didn't seem to pick up on Berg's tone, or if he did, he ignored it. "A rock was thrown through the window before the firebomb. It had a triangle chiseled into it. I'm Jewish myself, and I recognized it as a symbol the Nazis made Jews wear on concentration camp uniforms."

Berg wondered why an anti-Semitic firebomber would choose a symbol most people wouldn't even know about, rather than, say, a swastika or a Star of David. Maybe, he thought, because the bomber was too smart for his or her own good and just couldn't resist doing something subtle. Then Berg thought of something else, something that would expand the range of motives and suspects, which would mean that the bomber was just smart. "The Nazis did use a yellow triangle for Jews, but they used a pink one for homosexuals," he said. "And some gays and lesbians are using the symbol themselves now. Did anyone check out that angle?"

"Yeah, we did," the detective said, showing by the way he said it that he didn't appreciate a campus cop questioning whether his department knew what they were doing. "We caught that angle early on, and it seems to be a dead end. Neither Dr. Janovitz nor her husband is homosexual. We checked that out pretty thoroughly. And neither of them has been involved in any gay controversies, either for or against. Anyway, gay and lesbian issues haven't really hit here. It's pretty much a live-and-let-live place."

"Any suspects in the firebombing?"

"None. Dr. Janovitz has no ideas. Her husband has no ideas. We have no useful forensics or anyone to suspect ourselves."

"Any chance it was a disgruntled student, do you think, or maybe a neighbor they have a feud with, or someone who had something against the husband?"

"We checked. I myself talked to a professor who works with Dr. Janovitz. She is a department head and doesn't teach much. She could do other things to get students mad, but the professor said Dr. Janovitz is very well liked. You never can tell, but a student doesn't seem likely. Her husband is a partner in an accounting firm that does work for corporations. We've been able to smoke nothing helpful out there. We had patrol officers canvass the neighborhood, and we asked the Janovitzes about neighbors. None of them seem likely."

"Why do you think the bombing was mostly personal?" Berg said, wanting to be satisfied on the anti-Semitic angle.

"Because neither Dr. Janovitz nor her husband is a good symbol to pick on as a Jew. She's observant, but she doesn't wear her religion on her sleeve. Same with her husband. People say they don't talk about their religion unless it happens to come up—in fact, some of them didn't even know the family is Jewish. Plus, they don't live in a mostly Jewish neighborhood. That's one side of it. The other is that there are some out-front Jews in this town. One of the rabbis for starters. He's a militant Zionist. And there are others who could piss-off some Klan type with their interest in Jewish causes. I'm in a pretty good position to know the good candidates, and neither Dr. Janovitz nor her husband is one of them."

"So you think the Jewish angle was just a cover," Berg said.

"Maybe not just a cover, maybe the firebomber doesn't like Jews—or homosexuals for that matter, if we're wrong about that angle—but I'm convinced the house wasn't just a random Jewish or homosexual target."

Berg had heard enough to be convinced. "Do you mind telling me what happened?"

"No, if you don't mind telling me why you're interested."

Berg laughed. "Fair trade, you first."

"It happened about one o'clock Sunday morning. Dr. Janovitz wakes up to a loud crash and her eight-year-old daughter running into their bedroom, screaming and on fire. She and her husband smother the kid in the bedspread to get the fire on her clothes out. By then they can't even get out of their room by the door, because the hallway's on fire.

"The husband knocks out the bedroom window with a chair, helps his wife and daughter out, then jumps out himself. They were lucky to make it, but the daughter was badly burned. She's going to be in the hospital a long time. By the time the fire department got there, the whole back of the house was gone. They were able to save the front part, but I don't know if it'll pay to rebuild it."

"And you're sure it was a firebombing?"

"The fire marshal went through the next morning. There's no doubt. First there's the rock. Plus he found a broken bottle, which he says is the remains of a Molotov cocktail. I don't know much about those things, but he says that whoever did it knew how to get the job done. There were storm windows on the house, so he says it was smart to throw the rock through first, to make sure the firebomb got into the room. Also, he says most people make a Molotov cocktail using just gasoline, but that this one was a mixture of gasoline and kerosene. According to the fire marshal, that's the way it should be done. I don't know why."

Berg didn't know either.

"Your turn," the detective said.

"I believe I can tie your firebombing in with some murders. The problem is, I can't give you any evidence or a sure suspect. We've got a few suspects, with one at the top of the list. The firebombing just put him higher up."

"A name and why you think he did it is good enough for a start."

"The name is Gerald Duncan. He's a chemistry professor here. We suspect he killed his dean six months ago so he could replace him. The week before last, we think he killed a professor who he was competing against for a research prize that would help him get the deanship. Also, we expect that he killed a member of his dissertation committee fifteen years ago because the guy was giving him a hard time. I'd guess he firebombed the Janovitzes house to try to kill her. She's his main rival for the deanship he killed the two other people for. Or I should say 'may be his main rival,' because she doesn't know if she'll stay in the running."

"Is this guy a moron too?" the detective asked.

"What do you mean?" Berg said, wondering if he'd missed something.

"Well, two murders and one firebombing in six months that can all be tied together and dropped in one guy's lap seems a little obvious."

Berg hoped he hadn't missed anything, partly because he didn't want to look a fool. "Duncan's no moron. The murders were very slick and wouldn't have pointed to him—or anyone else at the university—if they had gone as planned. And they almost did."

"And the firebombing?"

"That doesn't seem too slick," Berg said, pausing to see if he had a decent answer for why Duncan would take that chance. Then it struck him. "No, that's not right. It was done before he knew we were looking at him or had even tied any of the murders together. It wouldn't have seemed too dangerous then."

"Still sounds a little desperate to me."

"I think you've hit on it," Berg admitted, sorry he hadn't thought of it himself. "The guy's getting desperate—assuming he's our killer."

Berg put down the phone and told Eve about what was looking like Jerry Duncan's maniacal quest for a deanship.

"WHAT ABOUT YOUR DEANSHIP?" SHE ASKED. "HAVE YOU THOUGHT more about it?"

"Yes, I have. A lot. It makes me feel sick to think about it. I don't want any part of it."

Eve put her arms around his neck. "I know that's the right choice," she said. Then she pulled his lips to hers.

Chapter Twenty-Four

THE PREVIOUS SATURDAY AFTERNOON, JUST A HALF AN HOUR BEFORE DARK, THE firebomber had arrived in the town where Dr. Janovitz lived. The bomber wasn't concerned about meeting her on the street. As an observant Jew, she wouldn't likely be out on a Saturday afternoon.

A drive down Janovitzes street turned up her house, the direction of travel chosen so that it would be on the passenger's side, making it unlikely that anyone could see the driver. After turning the first corner, the car moved down the closest side street and into the alley at the rear. While there was risk involved, it was necessary to check where the bedrooms were. The Janovitzes house was one story, and in the back were what looked like bedroom curtains on the windows of two rooms.

The bomber then drove to a town fifty miles away to spend the evening. Spaghetti and Italian sausage went down well with a glass of red wine—one glass only, to stay sharp. A local paper, bought from a rack outside, provided a movie guide. There was one that looked interesting, a love story between CIA and KGB agents. It was playing at a theater next to a mall. That sounded good, because some shopping was necessary. A discount store there provided cheap sports shoes and imitation leather gloves.

The bomber had already made the Molotov cocktail, two-thirds gasoline and one-third kerosene, with a rag for a fuse. It was in the trunk, cradled in newspapers inside a cardboard box, with the fuse out and a cap on the bottle. The bottle was already clean of fingerprints, on the one in a thousand chance that the bomb wouldn't destroy them. In the trunk there was also a rock, four inches in diameter.

When the mall closed, it was about time to watch the love story about spies. After the movie, enjoyed at least enough to stay awake, the bomber drank coffee and ate pumpkin pie in an all-night restaurant on the edge of town. In the parking lot, the new shoes went on for the fifty mile drive to Janovitzes house. The drive went slowly, because a traffic ticket would mean the end of the plan.

The bomber parked a block away from Janovitzes house, near the alley. There were no street lights near, and none in the alley. With gloved hands, the firebomb was taken from the trunk, along with the rock. After inserting the fuse, the bomber walked slowly down the alley, rock in one hand and firebomb in the other. Luckily, no dogs barked. By walking into Janovitzes backyard and creeping close to the house, it might have been possible to get a better look at the curtains at the back of the house to see which were adults' and which children's.

No such luck. It was too dark. The bomber put the firebomb on the ground and threw the rock through the nearest window, then picked up the firebomb, lit the fuse, and tossed it in after the rock.

Without waiting to see what happened, the bomber ran out of the backyard and then walked quickly down the alley and into the waiting car. Driving out of the neighborhood without going down Janovitzes street, it was impossible to be sure of success, but a loud "whoosh" had gone up as the gasoline-kerosene mixture ignited. The odds of success were good.

Chapter Twenty-Five

On Wednesday morning Berg awoke to the sound of a cold October rain hitting the roof of his bedroom. He got out of bed, rubbing his eyes, and shuffled to the window, his slippers only half on his feet. He saw that the rain was pouring "as if from a bucket," as a Russian professor had taught him to say.

"The Russians got that one right," he sighed.

Ginger got up from her place on the floor at the end of the bed and walked over to Berg, her tail wagging. She expected him to put on his clothes and take her to the fields.

"We can't go today," Berg said to her.

She seemed to understand, because her tail stopped wagging and her head drooped. Berg walked to the chair that sat near a window on the opposite side of the room and plopped down, still trying to shake off sleep. Ginger sat on the floor beside him and pushed her nose under his hand, asking to be petted.

As Berg sat stroking her head, Eve woke up. She was always pretty, but Berg found her to be especially pretty in the morning, with the freshness of sleep in her eyes.

"Good morning, Beautiful," he said when he saw she was awake.

"No walk this morning?" she asked.

"It's raining too hard. I'd freeze to death."

"You know you have to get exercise every morning," Eve said, smiling slyly. "I've got an exercise for you that's guaranteed to burn a hundred calories, if you do it right."

Berg kicked off his slippers and climbed back into bed, letting Eve pull him toward her.

BERG SAT AT THE BREAKFAST TABLE DRINKING ORANGE JUICE AND eating raisin bread toast as he went over his notes for the seminar on use of force he would give the university police that morning. He was running late and decided he'd work at home before going to the police building.

When he finished looking over his notes, he reached for the telephone on the wall next to the kitchen table.

"Our killer's tried it again," Berg told Kate when she picked up her phone.

"Who this time?"

"The outside candidate for dean. Didn't kill her, just burned her house and put her little daughter in the hospital. I'll tell you all about it when I see you. I've got to come over and give some training this morning. Can we get together afterward?"

"Sure," she said. "Come and see me when you're finished."

The Labcoat

Berg put down the phone and looked out the kitchen window. The rain had stopped, and he could see lighter sky to the west. "Too late," he said to Ginger, knowing she still wanted him to take her to the fields. "Maybe we can walk tonight."

BERG STRODE INTO THE TRAINING ROOM AT THE POLICE BUILDING and began greeting people in the assembled crowd, mostly patrol officers, as he moved toward the front of the room. He laid his attaché case on a table and took out his notes. He remembered well that when his ethics class had discussed the use of force his students had gotten mad about police who use too much force and about prosecutors who let them get away with it. Berg knew he wouldn't hear any of that from the police.

His plan was first to lecture and then answer questions. As he half-expected, it didn't work out that way, because some of the things he said, which came mostly from laws and court cases, the audience couldn't choke down without interrupting to protest.

"You mean if a guy threatens me with a bottle, I can't shoot him?" one of the newer officers asked, seeming incredulous. Berg wondered where the guy had been when use of force was covered in the training academy.

"It depends. Is your life in danger? How far away is he? Is he falling down drunk? Lots of things go into it."

"Like if he's a little guy I can't, but if he's a big guy I can?"

"I can't answer it that simply. Maybe he's a little squirt and stumbling around from too much beer, but he's a serial killer just escaped from prison. Maybe a court would say you'd be justified in shooting him rather than take the chance he'd kill you and get away."

"Maybe? Maybe? That's the problem. I'm out there taking a chance that some punk will hit me with a bottle and shoot me with my own gun, and you can't even tell me what I can do about it."

"Hey, don't kill the messenger," Berg said, throwing up his arms. "I'm just trying to tell you what the world is like out there. If you shoot someone when the rules say you shouldn't, it's your butt. I won't be able to help you and neither will anyone else around here. It'll be out of our hands."

AFTER THE TRAINING, BERG WENT TO KATE'S OFFICE AND TOLD her the details of the Janovitz firebombing.

"Duncan's the only one who had a reason to do all these crimes, but we don't have squat on him," Berg said, frustrated.

"So far as we know he's the only one with motives for all the crimes," Kate corrected, "assuming the fifteen-year-old murder wasn't a mob hit bought by his dissertation advisor's wife."

"You're right. I'm not thinking enough about motives," Berg said. Then, after a moment, he continued. "You know, I never really believed Lerner when he said he didn't want to be dean. He has become the consummate administrator, even in the way he dresses. I can't believe he wouldn't jump at the chance."

"But he doesn't seem to be in the running at the moment."

"You're right about that too, but who knows, maybe he thinks the provost will turn to him if the field narrows—which is where we're going. Or maybe he'd go after these people out of jealousy." Berg paused, then continued, "That's all pretty weak though." Then Berg went silent again, until he came up with a more likely thought. "You know, his problem with the government grants may have given him a good motive for Willard, Ellingham, and Janovitz."

"How so?" Kate said.

"We know Willard had a file on the grants, though we don't know whether Lerner knew that. Say he did and that Willard had gone to Ellingham with the information. For all we know, Ellingham may have already told Lerner he was going to fire him, or maybe Lerner was just afraid he would. That could account for both Willard and Ellingham."

"But the six-month wait to kill Willard is hard to see," Kate said. "It seems dangerous to have waited that long."

"Based on what we know. Maybe Lerner made promises to Willard that kept him from going to the interim dean during those six months—like promising to give him the research prize—but maybe he also didn't trust Willard to keep his mouth shut forever."

"Could have happened," Kate said, thoughtfully. "And Janovitz?"

"She's a little harder to fit in." Then after a little thought Berg went on. "But maybe not. Duncan probably knew at least something about what Lerner was doing with grant money, and he didn't do anything about it as far as we know. Maybe Lerner thought he would be safe with Duncan as dean, but feared Janovitz."

"So you really think he's a good suspect?" Kate said.

"No, not really, I'm just trying to keep my mind open. Lerner's way down the list compared to Duncan, and it's him we've got to pursue."

"We probably could get a search warrant for his condo and office," Kate offered. "We should be able to convince a judge that we have probable cause."

"I don't know what we could ask a judge to let us look for except weapons, and I'll lay any odds Duncan is too smart to keep them around."

"I suppose you're right," Kate said, then paused. Berg stayed quiet, letting her think. "Look," she went on, "Duncan seems to be losing control. Unless there are other murders we haven't been able to find, it looks like he went fifteen years between his first murder and Ellingham, then five months, and now a week. With a deanship decision coming soon, he seems to have a hair trigger."

"You mean we should watch him?" Berg asked.

"Why don't we see if we can spring his trigger while we watch him? If we can find something to set him off, maybe we can catch him in the act."

"And what if we're wrong about him?"

"Then his trigger won't spring," Kate said, shrugging her shoulders.

"It's got to be something about the deanship," Berg said as he got up to begin pacing. "That's what he's put all his energy into."

"It looks like everything he's done is to get someone out of the way, so it seems to me we should put someone new in his way," Kate suggested.

"What about the prize he killed Willard for," Berg said, not really making it a question. "I wonder if it's been put through yet. Here, let me have your phone. I'll call his chair and see." Lerner's secretary answered the phone, and Berg said, "Is Dr. Lerner in?"

"No, he's in a meeting."

"Well, look, what I need to know is, has he sent anyone's name forward for that research prize that Frank Willard and Jerry Duncan were in the running for? Do you know?"

"I haven't seen anything about it in a while. But I keep a calendar of dates when things are due around here. Let me check."

Berg could hear the rustling of papers as Lerner's secretary searched her calendar.

"Yes, I've got it here," she said after a few seconds. "The deadline is next week."

"Was that date announced, do you think?"

"I'm sure it wasn't. It's just between Dr. Lerner and the interim dean. It's up to Dr. Lerner who to put up for the prize."

"Okay, do me a favor, will you? When Dr. Lerner gets out of his meeting, ask him to call. It's very important." After giving the secretary Kate's number and hanging up the phone, Berg turned back to Kate. "Maybe we can get Lerner to put someone else's name in."

"He'd have to find someone who has the right credentials and who's willing to be a target," she told him, not seeming to think much of his idea.

"I guess it could be a mess," Berg said. "Plus, we couldn't be sure who Duncan would go after, Lerner or this new prize winner, so we'd have to watch two people."

"What about his putting Frank Willard in for the award posthumously?" Kate suggested, clapping her hands and then pointing at Berg. "That should freak Duncan out, and he can't kill Willard twice." She paused, seeming to think further. "No, it would be better if Lerner just said he was going to do it. Then maybe Duncan would go after him before he could go through with it."

"Yeah, that might work." It didn't seem nearly a sure thing to him, but he hadn't been able to come up with a better idea.

"We'd need to get Duncan to act fast," Kate said, eager to push her idea forward. "We couldn't watch Lerner carefully enough for very long."

"Lerner's secretary said the deadline for putting a name in isn't until next week, but that other people don't know that.

Lerner could call Duncan in today, late in the afternoon to give us time to prepare."

Kate picked up on his idea. "He could tell Duncan that he had decided to put Willard in for the prize posthumously, but could mention that he'll wait for the deadline to make it look like his decision went down to the wire. Like he's trying to throw Duncan a little bone."

"That sounds okay, I guess. He could say the deadline is, maybe, the end of the day Friday. That way Duncan would have to move by then."

"Wait a minute," she said. "We may really be screwing up here. Is Duncan the only inside candidate for the deanship?

"No," Berg said, stopping his pacing for a moment. "Eve told me there's one other internal candidate. A guy in the physics department."

"Well, there's a problem. What if Duncan decides to go after him instead of Lerner, just eliminate the inside competition and hope that Janovitz will drop out?"

"Maybe, but both Lerner and Eve told me Duncan is the favored inside candidate. I think Lerner would be the more likely target, at least for the next couple of days. The guy in physics wouldn't have to be eliminated immediately."

"Don't you think we'll have to watch the other candidate too, though?" Kate asked, concerned that Berg wasn't seeing a danger that was obvious to her.

"I guess you're right. Or maybe we can get him to go out of town for a couple of days. Look, I've got to go teach my eleven o'clock class. When Lerner calls, set up a meeting for as soon as you can."

Chapter Twenty-Six

BERG WALKED INTO HIS SECRETARY'S ROOM AFTER CLASS, BOOKS IN HAND AND just finishing a conversation with a student who had followed him from his classroom.

"Detective Michaelman wants you to call her," Irene told Berg when the student left.

"Anything else happening?"

"Nothing that won't wait."

Berg sunk down into his big leather chair and called Kate.

"Were you able to get anything set up?" Berg asked a few seconds later, now standing by the desk in his office, trying to extricate himself from his blazer with his one free hand.

"We can see Jim Lerner right after lunch. How about if I buy today? I can pick you up in a couple of minutes."

"You're on," Berg told her. After he hung up the telephone he wondered if he'd have the same erotic and yet uncomfortable feelings he'd had the last time they had lunch. So far he didn't, because Jerry Duncan was taking up too much space in his brain.

A good measure of Berg's preoccupation with Duncan was his relative lack of interest in Kate as he followed her to a table in the Hunan restaurant she took him to. She wore a clingy wool jersey skirt and looked like she had put on weight since she bought it. It fit tighter than most women would like, but not too tight for Berg.

The initials VPL came to his mind as he followed her between the tables. Visible Panty Line. He'd learned those initials in Vietnam, he supposed because during his year there someone in America had thought them up. Vietnam wasn't the most likely place for thinking up something for which there was little use. Much too little use, Berg remembered.

Kate glanced over her shoulder and saw Berg following along, his eyes focused on her. Berg caught her eyes and wondered if she was sorry not to see the appreciation he usually showed. He was looking, but he didn't appear to be much interested.

Chinese food was a favorite of Berg's, the hotter the better. They ordered dishes to share, the ones Kate ordered, and then began going over the plan for Lerner. They guessed that he would be willing to take some risk. Whether he would feel the same way about his family was another question.

"Do you think the chief can find some money for overtime?" Kate asked, knowing they would need extra patrol officers, probably working plainclothes.

"I'm sure he can. Plus, I think we'd better bring the city in on this. For one thing, we're going to have to borrow a wire and a communications van from them if we want to hear what goes on between Lerner and Duncan. We might as well ask for some bodies too."

An hour later they were in Lerner's office.

"You've heard about the firebombing of Dr. Janovitzes house?" Berg began.

"Yes, I heard yesterday."

"We believe that Jerry Duncan did it, plus killed Frank Willard and Stuart Ellingham. And a member of his dissertation committee when he was in graduate school."

"Are you sure?" Lerner asked skeptically.

"We feel sure, but not absolutely. And we can't prove it. We interviewed him yesterday. He was cool, but we both think he tripped himself up a couple of times."

"All this for a deanship?" Lerner asked.

"That's a lot when you consider the number of people who are killed for nothing," Kate told him.

"We've got a plan," Berg said, leaning forward in his chair and looking at Lerner closely. "It involves some danger. To you and your family, unless we can get them completely out of the way. But we need to get Duncan to make a move when we're watching if we're going to catch him."

"I'm willing. I don't know about involving my wife. Let me hear about it."

"Call him in this afternoon, say about five, and tell him you've decided to tell the interim dean to give the research prize to Willard posthumously. Say you're going to hold off talking to the dean until late Friday afternoon, because you intend to put out a memo to the department saying you delayed to the last minute because it was a hard choice. Tell him you hope he understands and so on. You know the lingo."

"What happens then?"

"We hope he'll come after you," Kate said. "He's already killed to get the prize, and if we read him correctly, he's about flipped out—probably more so now, since his firebombing hasn't eliminated the outside candidate, at least not yet. If he does come after you, we'll be ready."

"What we'd like you to do is move out of your house and let us move in, so that if he tries it at night, you won't be there," Berg added. "If your wife, and any children, could stay with friends day and night for the next two days, they should be out of danger completely."

"Well, my wife isn't working at the moment, and our children are off at college, so I don't think that will be a problem. We can stay at a hotel for a couple of days if necessary—at the university's expense."

"That would take care of the times you're away from the university," Berg said. "We'd just have to watch Duncan to see if he's following you. I think we can work that out. When you're here, we'll have you wired, provided we can get some help from the city police. Plus we'll have someone close." Berg paused, looking at Kate. "By the way, who is the professor in physics who's also in the running for the deanship?"

"Jim Carmichael," Lerner replied.

"I'm not too concerned that Duncan will go after him," Berg said, "but I should talk to him anyway."

Chapter Twenty-Seven

I'VE ALREADY HEARD ABOUT YOUR JERRY DUNCAN," THE CITY'S CHIEF OF DETECTIVES told Berg when he called that afternoon. "The department handling the Janovitz case called me first thing this morning. They asked us to interview Duncan's neighbors to see if they knew where he was Saturday night."

"Any luck?" Berg asked.

"Not so far, and I doubt we'll have any. Duncan lives in a condo complex, and he has his own attached garage. His neighbors say he keeps to himself mostly, and they can't see if his car is there. I don't think anyone is going to be able to say he was or wasn't home Saturday night."

"Did you get the picture of what we think Duncan has been up to?"

"I got a summary. How sure are you about these murders?"

"Pretty sure, but I need your help in trying to catch him. We're set to lay a trap if you're interested."

"If he's half what you think he is, I'm interested."

Berg filled the chief of detectives in on the plan and got his commitment for a wire and a communications van, so they could record everything said over the wire, plus a driver and a communications technician.

"Those we'll only need during certain times of the day, beginning later this afternoon through Friday. We're only going to let Duncan have access to Lerner for parts of each day, and those are the only times he'll need to be wired."

"Just during the day shift?"

"Right. Other times Lerner is going to disappear so we don't have to worry about protecting him. We're going to have his house staked out at night in case Duncan shows up. We're also going to want to put a tail on Duncan so we have some warning of what he's doing. I hoped maybe you could spare some people to help do that."

"I can for a couple of days, but that's about it."

"I'm with you. We've been planning to call it quits by five Friday if nothing has happened by then."

The two men arranged the details of how they would work together, including that the communications technician would meet Berg at the university police station at a quarter after four to set up the wire on Lerner, and that a detective would put a watch on Duncan's car beginning at five.

Berg left Kate to work out the other details of the plan while he went to teach his three o'clock class. He promised Kate that he would take care of calling Duncan's rival for the deanship.

At five o'clock, Berg was sitting in the back of the communications van with a headset on, ready to listen when Lerner told

Duncan his plan for the research prize. Kate was in an empty office down the hall from Lerner, ready to move if she got the word by handheld radio. Berg didn't expect trouble. Mostly this was a dry run to test out the communications setup, although there was a hope that Duncan would say something incriminating, so the tape began rolling as soon as he walked into Lerner's office.

The meeting turned up nothing. Duncan wasn't happy to hear what Lerner planned, but he showed his unhappiness just by being morose.

Two hours later, Berg and Kate were sitting in Lerner's house starting to eat a pizza.

"Damn," he said as hot cheese hit the top of his mouth. "I hoped things would get hot around here tonight," he joked with a sly smile, "but not like that."

"Dream on," Kate said.

A couple of minutes later they got a call on their handheld. It was the city detective assigned to follow Duncan.

"Unit four to unit six. He's in his car now, moving."

"Roger four. Let us know if he's coming our way."

"I'll do it."

Five minutes passed. Silence from the radio.

"Unit six. He may be headed your way. Can't tell for sure. He's not going home though."

"Roger. Did he carry anything into his car with him?"

"Yeah. A box."

Another five minutes passed.

"Unit six. I think he's coming your way, all right. Either that or to another house in that subdivision. He'll be there in another minute if he's coming."

"Okay. We'll watch for him."

Berg went into the dining room and Kate into a front bedroom. Those rooms were dark, but they left the living room lights on so the house would look occupied. They each looked out a corner of their windows, guns drawn. The guns were, they knew, just whistling in the dark. The only bad thing they could expect at this point was a firebomb, and a .38 wasn't going to do them much good against that.

"Unit six, he's turned on your street and he's slowing down. I'm going to have to fall back if I don't want him to see me."

"Okay," Kate said. "We're watching. I'll tell you what I see. Here comes a car."

"He's going by," Kate said, relieved but a little disappointed too.

"Okay six, I can see his tail lights. I'll pick him up again."

"What do you suppose he was doing?" Berg asked as they went back into the living room.

"The only thing I can think of is, he's planning another firebomb."

A minute later they got another radio call.

"Unit four to unit six. He's pulled into the driveway of a house a couple of blocks down from you. There are no lights in the house."

"Keep us informed unit four."

"I'm doing the best I can without being made."

Another minute passed.

"Unit four to unit six. He walked to the door and knocked. Now he's just standing there." After a half minute, "Okay, he's getting back in his car, and I can see his backup lights coming on." After a few more seconds the city detective spoke again. "I'm following again. I'll let you know if anything happens."

"Thanks unit four."

Berg and Kate sat at the kitchen table, the radio between them. They didn't feel like small talk, so just listened for a radio call, eating pizza again. Ten minutes later it came.

"Unit four to unit six. He's home now. Car's in the garage."

"Unit six to unit five," Berg said. "Can you see his front door?"

"Roger."

"And four, do you have good cover for the back of his place?"

"Roger, no problem. We're going to be here all night. Sleep tight."

Berg noted the jealous tone in "sleep tight." He couldn't blame the guy. Berg was holed up in a nice house with an attractive woman, and all the city detective had to look forward to was a lonely night in his car.

"What in the hell was that all about?" Kate asked.

"I have no idea. Maybe a drive by to check out Lerner's house and maybe nothing."

"Well, we are on the edge of the ghetto," Kate said. "He could have a lot of friends around here."

"Yeah, but on the other hand, I don't believe in coincidences." Berg paused. "At least not much," he added, knowing that the drive-by might have been coincidental.

"He may have picked up the tail," Kate said. "If so, he sure thought fast."

"That's what I'd expect from Duncan," Berg said, furrowing his brow while trying to decide what to say. "Do you think we can trust those guys to stay awake?" he said.

"Probably."

"That's what I think. And it isn't good enough."

Lerner's wife had left a note saying the master bedroom on the first floor and the guest bedroom upstairs had fresh linen on the beds, but the thought of sleeping on the first floor wasn't appealing, considering what had happened to the Janovitzes. Berg and Kate both thought that if Duncan struck again with a firebomb, he would throw it downstairs. So they decided to take turns sleeping upstairs.

"Do you want the first shift or the second?" Berg asked Kate.

"I'd rather stay up."

"Okay, wake me around two or three and I'll take over.

AS DUNCAN CAME INTO HIS CONDOMINIUM FROM THE GARAGE, THE first thing he did was step outside the front door and pull the mail out of his box. While Duncan was still in the entryway, his neighbor walked up the front steps.

"What have you been doing, Jerry?" the neighbor asked, trying to sound funny, but seeming accusatory. "The police were here earlier asking about you."

"What for, did they say?" Duncan asked.

"My wife talked to them. She just said they asked a lot of disjointed questions, none of which she had an answer to."

"Oh well, who knows? Thanks for telling me."

As soon as Duncan got back inside, he threw the mail down and began pacing.

"Berg," he said. "That son of a bitch Berg."

Chapter Twenty-Eight

THURSDAY MORNING AT SEVEN, BERG WAS SITTING IN THE LIVING ROOM WITH a cup of tea in hand, still trying to hold off sleep, when he got a radio call.

"Unit six, you there?"

"Roger, I'm here."

"He's driving out of his garage."

"Roger. Thanks. Keep me advised."

Nothing happened for ten minutes. Berg wondered if he should wake Kate, but decided not to until he knew Duncan was coming their way.

"Okay six. It looks like he's going to school. You can relax."

"Roger. Thanks."

DURING THE DAY, A LOOSE WATCH WAS KEPT ON DUNCAN—BY university police when he was in the chemistry building, and by city police when he left in his car. He spent most of the day at the university, leaving only for shopping and lunch at midday.

Lerner stayed out of the chemistry building except when Duncan was teaching, and for three hours in the afternoon, beginning at two o'clock. During those three hours, both Berg and Kate stood by in a room down the hall from Lerner's office, and Lerner was wired and monitored from the communications van. Berg, Kate, and Lerner all wore Kevlar vests, borrowed from the City Police, under their street clothes.

The plan was that if Duncan went to Lerner's office, Berg and Kate would move to the waiting room where Lerner's secretary usually sat, ready to spring into Lerner's office the instant they got a certain message over the radio. The message was "go! go!" If they heard those words, they were to go in, guns drawn.

But the call never came. At five o'clock, Lerner was surreptitiously escorted to his car and sent to join his wife at a hotel, and Berg and Kate drove to Lerner's house to spend their second night. At about eight, they heard their call sign on the radio.

"Unit six, this is unit four. He's in his car."

"Roger four. Thanks."

Ten minutes passed while Berg and Kate waited for further word.

"Unit six. He's stopped at Kroger's. I'll be out of the car."

"Roger."

Seven minutes passed.

"Unit four to unit six. Be on your toes. I've lost him."

"What happened?" Berg said, his stomach starting to knot.

"He went into the pharmacy that's connected to the store, and I waited for him to come out. He went out the pharmacy's door instead. By the time I caught on, his car was gone."

"Do you think he made you?"

"Don't know."

"Roger. We'll keep a lookout here. Unit five, are you set up at the condo?"

"Affirmative."

"How about getting to where you can see if he drives into his garage?"

"Yeah, good idea. I'll let you know if he shows up."

"Unit six to unit four. Why don't you come over close to us so we can get backup if we need it."

"Roger. I'm on my way."

Berg kept a lookout at the front of the house and Kate at the back. It was getting dark, and they couldn't see much, even with the lights off in the rooms they were in. Berg had taken the front of the house without considering that the back was by far the more dangerous. They'd brought one shotgun, a Benelli M3 Super Combo with one twelve-gauge shell in the chamber and seven in the magazine, double ought buckshot. It was just the weapon to have, but it was in the wrong place. Berg had it in the front with him.

He had felt his heart pick up speed as soon as he took his position by the window, and as the night got darker, he could feel himself begin to sweat.

"What a mess," he mumbled. "We're sitting ducks."

Berg hadn't felt these sensations since Vietnam. Vietnam was better than this, he told himself. At least we'd have had mines set up with tripwires.

"Unit six to unit four," Berg said into the radio.

"Go ahead."

"Do you see anything?"

"No. All quiet."

"Where are you?"

"Parked across the street, one house down."

"Can you see the front of the house pretty well?"

"Yeah. Pretty well."

"All right. Keep watching from there. Kate's looking out the back, but we can't see diddly out the windows. I'm going to go outside, out the back door. If you see anyone moving around out front, it isn't me."

"Roger. Be careful."

Berg walked to the window where Kate was.

"We've got to have someone outside," he said. "I'll try my best to stay out of your line of fire. Cover whatever window you think best. Here, you take the radio."

"Just don't be lighting any matches outside," Kate said, joking, "because I'm definitely going to shoot."

Berg opened the back door slowly and listened. He crouched low and scooted out the door, going between the shrubbery and the house. He stopped and waited halfway between the back door and the window where Kate had been. Within a few minutes his heart wasn't going as fast, and he had stopped sweating. This too was like Vietnam, but it felt good. His eyes had acclimated to the dark, and his hearing was finely tuned. He had good cover and a weapon he trusted. He was in control. A hunter, not the hunted.

He stayed there, crouched, half an hour. Then Kate stuck her head out the door.

"Duncan's back home."

"Great," Berg said with disgust, getting up and brushing dirt and pieces of dried leaves off his clothes. He had thought their investment was paying off. "Why don't you hit the sack first? I'll wake you when it's your turn."

Pushed by the strong sexual stimulant of shared danger, Kate ignored what he said and put her hand lightly on his chest as he came in the back door. "I think we can trust the surveillance for a couple of hours," she said quietly. Berg, feeling the same effect, put his arm around her shoulders as they walked toward the upstairs guest room.

Chapter Twenty-Nine

"Oh come on, lazy bones, wake up," Kate said to Berg as she stood by the edge of the bed. "I've got some orange juice poured and toast ready to be made."

"What time is it?" Berg asked, rubbing his eyes.

"Eight o'clock. Duncan's already at work. Drove straight there this morning."

Berg got up, wearing only his undershorts, and went to wash up. Fifteen minutes later he came into the kitchen, shaven and dressed. Kate was bending over the table, laying out breakfast.

"Last night," Berg began, and then paused. "We shouldn't have—" He paused again, not knowing what to say. "I didn't mean to," he finally added.

Kate turned around slowly. "Let's resolve to behave ourselves. Except," she added, trying to joke, "maybe when we have to spend the night together again."

Berg nodded and slumped in a chair at the table. A weakness in his stomach told him he didn't look forward to facing his wife.

"Are we square on the plan for today?" Kate asked, forcing both of them to get back to work.

"I think so. Lerner is supposed to be out of his building until two again. The city is going to keep a watch on Duncan's car and be ready to follow him if he drives away. What do you want to do?"

"It's almost impossible to watch him when he's inside the chemistry building. There is no place to watch from. Until two o'clock, I think about all we can do is stay around the building and make sure Lerner's office isn't left open for Duncan to get at. I can do that, and maybe I'll spend some time helping watch his car. It wouldn't hurt to have two of us following Duncan if he drives someplace."

"You're right about that. Look, I have to teach my eleven o'clock class. Let's meet in your office at about a quarter to two."

FIVE MINUTES BEFORE BERG'S CLASS WAS SCHEDULED TO LET OUT, Berg's phone rang.

"Hello. This is Jim Lerner," the man said to Berg's secretary when she picked up the phone. "Please tell Chief Berg to meet me in Frank Willard's office as soon as he gets out of class. It's very important. Tell him I've discovered something he has to see right away."

"I'll give him the message," she said. "He'll be back in a few minutes."

Berg walked in ten minutes later, still thinking about the night before and filled with guilt—for what he had done and over his fantasies about Kate, which he'd been feeding for weeks, thinking, like a little boy, that he could play with matches and not get burned.

"Jim Lerner called," Berg's secretary said, interrupting his thoughts as she passed on the message.

Berg wondered why Lerner was in the chemistry building when he wasn't supposed to be there until two o'clock, but he wondered more what Lerner could have found. Something that would incriminate Duncan, he hoped. But he also wondered if it might be something altogether different, something that would exonerate Duncan instead. Since his trap was coming up empty, Berg began to wonder if he'd been as wrong about Duncan as he'd been about himself.

Berg pulled his car into the chemistry building's parking lot, maneuvering as usual to miss potholes. He got out and walked toward the stairs leading to the front door of the building. Twelve o'clock classes had already started, and the noon lunch crowd had left minutes ago, so no one else was near the front door.

As Berg's foot hit the bottom step, a man walked through the front door and started down. Six steps separated the men when Berg looked up and saw the man headed toward him, swinging a newspaper in his left hand. He was moving quickly, but to Berg he seemed to be moving much slower than he really was. Suddenly everything seemed to be moving slowly.

Berg brushed his right hand across the center button of his sports coat, unfastening it, as the man made it to the next step. As Berg began to bend his knees into a crouch, he threw the tail of his coat aside, grabbed the handle of the revolver on his right hip, and at the same time disengaged the holster's quick-release strap with his right thumb.

By the time the man had made it down another step, Berg's gun had cleared his holster and was on its way forward. A fraction of a second later Berg had his arms straight out, gun in a two-handed grip, and he began pulling the trigger. Rapid fire, three shots aimed at the center of the man's chest. The man staggered back under the force of three .38 caliber hollowpoint slugs tearing through his sternum.

Berg had acted with pure animal instinct, but now his mind started working for the first time since his hand had touched the button of his coat. Everything sped up now. His mind raced, as if nature were trying to balance out the physics of time. He heard the prosecutor who had met with his class saying, "The guy panicked and forgot all his training. There wasn't any question that I'd prosecute him." Berg heard himself saying, "If you shoot someone when the rules say you shouldn't, it's your butt." Berg had seen no weapon, given no warning.

"So much for rules," he mumbled to himself.

As Kate ran around the corner of the building, gun in hand, Jerry Duncan crumpled on the steps and then, propelled by gravity, fell headlong to the bottom of the stairs, his white labcoat trailing out behind him. As he began his fall, his newspaper dropped from his hand. The newspaper hit a step, and out of it tumbled a five-inch metal tube.

Chapter Thirty

DUNCAN HAD FALLEN WITH HIS HEAD TURNED TO THE RIGHT, HIS FACE POINTING AT the sun. Kate knelt and pushed hard with her fingers on the side of his throat, feeling for a pulse. Nothing. She lifted his eyelid with her right hand and slowly waived her left over the eye, shielding it from the sun. The pupil stayed fixed, the eye staring straight ahead.

Berg stood and watched, a blank expression on his face, his mouth half open. Kate saw that his right index finger was still inside the trigger guard of his gun.

"Eric," she said softly, putting her hand on his shoulder, "take your finger off the trigger." When he did, she added, "Hand me the gun." Berg gave it to her, his expression unchanged.

Depressing the "talk" button on her portable radio, Kate said, "Dispatch, this is Detective One. Send all the patrol people you can spare to the chemistry building for crowd control, and call city homicide. Tell them we've got an officer-involved shooting, with the bad guy down for good."

"Snap out of it, Eric," Kate said, as she put her hand under his chin and turned his face toward hers. She smiled and added, "Everything's okay."

Seeing the sparkle in Kate's eyes, Berg's mind began to wake up.

"It almost wasn't," he said, looking down at Duncan's weapon and realizing how close he'd come to having the wrong end of it explode in his face.

"Doesn't matter," Kate said, squeezing his shoulder. "You're alive. That's what matters."

Bystanders had begun to gather, and two university police cars arrived, prompting Berg to take charge of controlling the scene until the homicide detectives got there ten minutes later. By then he was as close to his ordinary self as it was possible to be with a bloodstream full of adrenaline.

He told his story and Kate her's. A clean shoot, the city detectives said. The big problem, which no one knew the answer to, was what to do with Duncan's weapon. No one had any idea how it worked, so they didn't know what would set it off. They finally settled on putting it inside a sealed plastic evidence bag, inside another sealed plastic evidence bag, and delivering it to the crime lab for the forensic technicians to worry about.

As Kate and the city detectives began, slowly and carefully, to slide the aluminum cylinder into its first plastic bag, Eve ran down the path from the biology building, her labcoat flapping around her legs. Berg caught her in his arms and kissed her, brushed tears from her cheeks, and, with his arm around her, walked her to his car.